About the Author

Vin lives a quiet life in the Midwest with his partner and their puggle who pushes sass and entitlement to a new level. One day they will have a small farm or a cabin in the woods.

Hezekiah

Corvin Runda

Hezekiah

Olympia Publishers
London

www.olympiapublishers.com
OLYMPIA PAPERBACK EDITION

Copyright © Corvin Runda 2023
Cover illustration Luisa Galstyan

The right of Corvin Runda to be identified as author of
this work has been asserted in accordance with sections 77 and 78 of
the Copyright, Designs and Patents Act 1988.

All Rights Reserved

No reproduction, copy or transmission of this publication
may be made without written permission.
No paragraph of this publication may be reproduced,
copied or transmitted save with the written permission of the publisher,
or in accordance with the provisions
of the Copyright Act 1956 (as amended).

Any person who commits any unauthorised act in relation to
this publication may be liable to criminal
prosecution and civil claims for damage.

A CIP catalogue record for this title is
available from the British Library.

ISBN: 978-1-80439-326-0

This is a work of fiction.
Names, characters, places and incidents originate from the writer's
imagination. Any resemblance to actual persons, living or dead, is
purely coincidental.

First Published in 2023

Olympia Publishers
Tallis House
2 Tallis Street
London
EC4Y 0AB

Printed in Great Britain

Dedication

This book is dedicated to Kit, the first person to see me.

PART ONE

One

The first time that I remember one of the unusual things that happened wasn't actually the first time. I know that because I clearly remember the interaction with my mom. The first time that I do remember would have been between '83 and '87. I am not good with dates and ages, but I can usually narrow things down a bit. My mom moved us to Iowa in '87 and this took place when we still lived in California, so definitely before the summer of '87. It also happened at school, so that would have been after I started kindergarten in '83. It was closer to the '83 side of the range than '87. The whole thing about this being the first time I remember while not actually being the first time will be a little clearer when I explain what happened.

My mom picked me up after the school day had ended. Like most of the parents she came directly to my classroom just before the bell rang. The other children left quickly with their parents, those who did not, went directly to the bus for drop off. My mom and I were a little delayed because my teacher wanted to talk to her about my reading level. Not in a bad way, she believed I was an advanced reader. She had some recommendations she wanted to encourage my mom to get for me from the library.

We left the classroom and walked out by the playground. It didn't feel hot, so it was probably fall or winter. It's hard to remember that kind of detail. In many places you just need to think about what the sky and trees looked like to narrow down a season. In California, the sky was always blue and the trees always green. The only thing that really helps is to try and remember how hot it was. Summers were brutal, mostly the rest of the year was tolerable.

The playground was huge but some of the equipment, like the jungle gym and monkey bars, were on the side we were walking past. I looked out to the playground and immediately zeroed in on two children playing on the monkey bars. I didn't know them too well, my school was huge, I didn't know most of the others who went there. I had two good friends, Damian and Trevor, the rest were pretty non-descriptive to me. Anyway, I didn't know who they were, but I did know what was about to happen to one of them. I must have had a sad expression because my mom asked me what was wrong.

"The girl, she's going to lose her grip on the bars and fall. She's going to get hurt. Bad."

I didn't hesitate in telling her, back then I still trusted her. I was stupid.

She raised an eyebrow and gave me a half smirk. Then she heard the scream. The girl had fallen, she was holding her arm. It didn't really look like an arm any more. More like a snake flapping around trying to escape her grasp. Before my mom could react, a teacher appeared and scooped her up taking her somewhere else. We just stood there, my mom in shock, me just waiting for her to start walking again.

"You can never do that again," she whispered.

I looked up at her and didn't recognize her expression. It was the first time I'd looked at my mom and felt that way. She was standing right next to me, still looking at the monkey bars, but it was like she was gone. I could see her, but whatever existed behind her eyes was gone. Then, slowly, something else filled in the empty space. Her eyes lit with a fiery anger I had not seen in her before.

"That's Satan's power! You will never do that again and you will never talk about that again!"

No more whispering, she was yelling at me through clenched teeth, frothed spittle flying from her lips. I should have kept my mouth shut, but I was young, stupid, and rapidly becoming more and more confused by the situation.

"It's not Satan. It's just this thing that happens sometimes. It's not bad, it just happens. Sometimes I see something good that's going to happen and sometimes I see something sad."

I thought we were just having a normal mother and son conversation. I didn't recognize that what I was talking about wasn't normal. I should have known from her eyes that wasn't the case. Her eyes were boring through me. Or, maybe it's more accurate to say they didn't see me. That's it, she was staring at me, but at the same time didn't see me. Slowly she reached for her right hand with her left. She wore this ring on her hand. It was silver with a big blue stone in the middle. She twisted the ring until the stone was on the palm side. Without hesitation she raised her hand above my head and brought it straight down. I didn't have any idea at all that she would ever do something like that to me, so it didn't occur to me to move. I heard a loud cracking noise. I didn't immediately feel pain, it was more like a lightning bolt of ice shooting from the point of impact down my spine. The pain slowly bloomed on my skull. It was then that I screamed.

Another teacher came running out to ask what was wrong. I was holding the top of my head and still screaming, a mix of tears and snot running down my face. I wasn't screaming words, more just that generic scream that children do when they are hurt, or scared, or confused.

My mom grabbed my arm and said, "He fell, he's fine." Then she started dragging me away.

We didn't have a car so we walked home. My younger brother was too young for school, so he was staying with neighbors while Mom got me. My two older brothers were allowed to find their own way home, so it was just me and her.

By the time we were past the playground I had stopped screaming, though the sniveling and dripping snot continued for quite a while. About halfway home she changed again. It was like a tape recording of her earlier change, but in reverse. That time I watched closely. I watched the fire drain, then I saw the hollowness in her, then my mom came back. My normal mom. The version of her I had always known. She started talking to me like everything was normal and nothing had happened. I don't remember the specifics at that point, but I think she asked me if I had enjoyed my day. I remember being hesitant to respond, but I did respond. This other version of her was new to me and I didn't know what would cause her to come back. I remember a vague feeling of being withdrawn for a few days after that. I don't remember anything more specific.

Two

The second time didn't involve my mom, and it didn't involve anyone else. We still lived in California, so again it was before the summer of '87, but it was after the playground incident. It was night and everyone was asleep. We rented a two-bedroom house on Cecelia Street in the town of Callow. I shared a bedroom with my younger brother, my two older brothers shared a bedroom, and my mom slept on the couch in the living room.

I woke up. I wasn't scared awake or anything. I didn't have a nightmare, I didn't hear a noise, it was just one of those things. One minute I was asleep, the next I was awake. It happened all the time. That would turn out to be the first of many times I couldn't get back to sleep. My bed was against the wall farthest from the door. Facing the door from my bed, my brother's bed was along the right wall. There was a window by the wall my bed was against and another by the left wall. On the other side of my brother's wall was the living room. Sharing the wall with the door was our closet. Our dresser was underneath the window of the left wall. My mom didn't work so our family didn't have money which means we didn't have toys. That also means there was nothing else on the floor of our bedroom. Just open space.

I opened my eyes and standing right in the middle of our bedroom was a woman. At first, I thought it was Mom. My eyes adjusted to the moonlight. We didn't have a night light, but we slept with the blinds of both windows open. It wasn't my mom. The woman was dressed in a large, black dress. That kind that flows out at the bottom. It looked very lacey. Now I know to describe it as *Victorian*, but at that time I wasn't familiar with that word. Her hair was white and done in two large buns on top of her head. Not on the sides like *Princess Leia*, these sat side by side on the top of her head. She had a sheer black veil draped over her face that hid her features, but I could see the paleness of her skin. I've always thought that I'm one shade from albino, but this woman made me look tanned.

She just stood there looking at me. I remember very well that I had never been so frightened in my life, up until that point at least. I was still lying on my side with my head on my pillow. I tried screaming. My mouth was open and I was making all of the expressions for a scream, but nothing was coming out. It was like my throat was so tight, like the rest of my body, that I couldn't open it wide enough to get air through. My body was seized. I couldn't consciously move, though I was shaking enough that my tiny wooden bed was rattling.

She just kept looking and I just kept silently screaming, my eyes bulging. This went on for what felt like hours but looking back was more likely a minute at most. Then, she just disappeared. She didn't fade, there wasn't a flash, she didn't walk away. She was there and then she wasn't there.

It would be easy enough to say I was just having a bad dream, but if that was a dream I still haven't woken up. I stayed up the rest of that night, laying on my side, not moving. Even after she disappeared, I couldn't move. It took some time for the physical reaction to the fear to wear off. That was the start of my insomnia.

Three

Around that same time my mom became obsessed with the news. It didn't matter whether it was local, national, or global, if it was on, she was watching it. She'd become particularly obsessed with a story about a local serial rapist and killer the news was calling the Nightstalker. He'd hit in our area recently and my mom began to believe she would be one of his next targets. Previously we would have the blinds open in our bedrooms and living room at night, often we'd have the windows open too. We didn't have central air, so there was no heating or cooling. Opening the windows was the best we could do. Once her fear of the Nightstalker started, all the windows and doors had to be shut and locked, and each of the blinds had to be lowered.

My two older brothers weren't allowed to walk home from school by themselves any more. My younger brother wasn't allowed to stay at the neighbors when Mom would come get us from school either. She would bring him and then all five of us would walk home together. It was the same deal in the morning to get to school. At the time it didn't make sense to me. The Nightstalker didn't attack young boys, so I didn't get why we all had to walk together this way. Looking back, she was probably thinking more about her safety than ours. She probably thought he wouldn't possibly attack her with four children surrounding her. I mentioned before that Mom didn't have a job, so she had all the time she needed to become a paranoid wreck.

Before the Nightstalker, and other than the time at the

playground after school, my mom always seemed happy. She loved us and we loved her. We didn't have much, but she'd raised us to value each other more than things. We were close and supportive and knew when something was wrong with one of us. We all knew something was wrong with Mom. Bad things always happened, and the news always reported on them. She had never reacted like this before. She was always sullen; all she would talk about was the Nightstalker. He was a constant subject of conversation. We were just children and I know it was not appropriate to discuss the grisly details with us, but she couldn't stop. When her friends or our friends would come by, it was still all she could talk about. My two friends stopped coming over around then. I still hung out with them, I just had to meet them elsewhere.

Mom became laxer with taking care of the house too. Things had always been tidy and clean, but then she stopped cleaning. One time she forgot to make dinner. We tried to tell her, but she wouldn't look away from the TV. She was hollow again when she'd look at the TV. That night we were so hungry by the time we went to bed that my younger brother and I were both crying. It finally seemed to hit her that she hadn't fed us. If she were rational, she would have gone and made some food, sandwiches or something, for all of us. Instead, she looked me squarely in the eyes and told me that my hunger was just in my imagination. That if I told myself I had eaten I could convince my body of it and I wouldn't be hungry any more. Then, she made me pretend to hold a hamburger, and I had to eat it in front of her. She had that look again, the fiery one from the playground, so I didn't hesitate. The whole thing took around ten minutes. I had to hold it, take small bites, pretend to chew and swallow, while trying to make noises like there was actually food in my mouth. After I finished the farce, she made me thank her for the food she'd given me. My brother was watching us the entire time. I couldn't make out his expression and he didn't make a noise.

After she was done with me, I thought she would do the same to him. She didn't. She kissed him on the forehead, told him she loved him, said goodnight, and walked out of the room.

My nerves were shot. During the 'hamburger dinner' I believed she was going to hit me again. I was terrified. When it was over, I was exhausted. Probably from a mix of fear and not having any real food. I fell asleep quickly.

I had odd dreams that night. They started off normal enough, well, normal enough for a young child who was both worried about and scared of his mom. The beginning of the dream is still clear, but then it gets a little foggy. It started with me finding a large beast. Not the size of a house or anything, but maybe twice the size of a large bear. It was built more like a cat than a bear, but its mouth had been pulled forward, elongated like an alligator. It was covered in black fur and had paws that seemed too large for its body. It was just sitting in a large open space; I knew it was waiting for me. The ground was flat, dry, cracked dirt. Sort of red, but still sort of brown too. There were no trees, hills, or mountains around, nothing on the horizon. It was dark, but I could still see, even though I didn't see any source of light. Its eyes were grey. Not just the irises, but the entirety of both eyes. They didn't glow, they didn't sparkle, and even with a lack of pupils to identify direction, I could tell they were staring directly at me.

It didn't talk, and I didn't know if it could understand me, but I asked it to come with me, to guard my mom and my family from the Nightstalker. We needed protection. My mom wasn't well and I wanted her to be well and safe. That's when I woke up, but only for a few minutes.

This was when the mix of dream and reality got foggy. I didn't really see anything, but I heard a lot of commotion. Things running above me. I heard whispered talking. I heard bells, but those bells became loud sirens. I heard men talking, not my brothers, but grown men. I heard crying.

I woke up again. I expected to see the Dark Woman, but she wasn't there. Neither was my brother. Our room was all blue and red, flashing lights. I jumped out of bed and ran for Mom. She wasn't on the couch in the living room. I ran to my two older brothers' bedroom and they were both gone as well. I started yelling. I didn't know where anyone was. Then I noticed the flashing lights were coming through all the blinds. I ran to the front window of the living room and saw police cars outside; they had large lights shining on our roof. My mom and my brothers were standing on the sidewalk in front of our house. Most of our neighbors were there as well.

I threw open the front door and ran outside. I ran straight to my mom and put my arms around her legs, squeezing to hold on.

She looked down at me and asked, "Why are you out of bed?"

She was hollow again. I told her that I woke up and everyone was gone and I was scared and I saw everyone outside. My brothers just stood there looking at me. Mom told me to go back to bed.

One of the police officers intervened. "Ma'am, let's keep all your children out here until we've cleared the house."

I don't have the creative skills to describe the look she gave that officer, but I feel that if she thought she could take his gun and kill him right there, she would have. Still, she didn't say anything, she just stood and glared.

The officer didn't seem to know what to do or say at that point, so he just walked over to a group of officers and they started talking in hushed tones. They walked into the house and after a while came strolling out. They'd given their all clear. Two of them came back inside with my mom and my brothers. We were put back to bed, but I could hear the police in the living room with my mom. I couldn't make out the exact words, but I could tell my mom was being harsh with them and they were getting angry. I heard the door slam and then heard their car pull away.

My bedroom door opened and my mom stood in the doorway. The hallway light was on behind her, so she looked like a large, dark, Mom-shaped shadow in the door. She just stared. My eyes teared. I didn't understand what was going on. I was confused. I didn't understand anything that had happened that night, didn't know why my mom was just standing there glaring at me. The door creaked shut and I heard her steps on the wooden floor heading back to the living room.

The next day I learned more about what had happened. It was on the news. It turned out the neighbors called the police because they saw a man dressed in black on our roof. We had an unfinished attic which had one window on the front of the house. The neighbors said they saw a man fiddling with that window, trying to get inside. The person being interviewed went quiet, so the reporter started urging him to go on. The neighbor said they didn't really understand what they saw, but that there appeared to be someone or something else on the roof. That the other person, or thing, jumped at the man, and the man nearly fell off the roof. He caught himself before toppling down and dragged himself back up. He ran to the side of the house and jumped to the neighboring roof. The thing jumped after him. From there it was too dark for the neighbor to see anything. He'd already told his wife to call 911.

They cut to a video of the front of our house in daylight and the reporter elaborated on the details, how the police believed this was an attempted break-in from the Nightstalker, but that a vigilant neighbor must have seen what was going on and jumped on the roof to scare him away. My hollow mom just stared at the TV.

Still not adept at dealing with these situations, I looked at her and asked, "Why didn't you wake me up? You got everyone else. Someone was trying to break into our house. Why did you leave me in here alone?"

Without taking her eyes off the screen, her monotone response was, "You're from the devil."

Four

I was born in Meribald, Iowa, but before I was a year old my mom left my dad and moved me and my older brothers to California. At the time, she was pregnant with my younger brother. She had no friends or relatives in California, she just wanted a fresh start. I don't know all the details, but from what she had shared with us, our dad cheated on her and her family had disowned her. She never went into detail about why they disowned her, just that it had happened.

Once we were in California, she got involved with this religion called God's Own, a worldwide organization headquartered out of Washington state. God's Own had broken into territories. Each territory got a traveling overseer. Each territory also had around two dozen individual congregations. It can be a little confusing because the individual groups are called congregations, but so are the buildings the groups meet in, so the congregation (group of people), meet inside a congregation (building). Those individual congregations have their own overseer. The overseer would assign a body of drudges. All of those drudges are men and each have specific duties. Once you are baptized in God's Own, you are a brother or sister. Non-baptized could still attend the meetings, they just wouldn't technically be members.

Our congregation in California was great. The people were all nice. They took the religion seriously, but they were kind and considerate people. They helped our family a lot. I think they felt bad for a single mom with four boys and no income. We were accepted unquestionably, and Mom was baptized soon after joining. Those who were not part of God's Own were called Worldly. We weren't to associate with Worldly people. What that meant to the congregation in California was that we wouldn't seek to be friends with those outside of God's Own. We could still interact with Worldly people, but most of the adults weren't actively social with them.

I don't know what she was going off to do, but often our mom would leave us with members of God's Own. Since we didn't have a car, they would pick us up in the morning and then drop us off in the afternoon or evening. Our congregation was fairly large, around 200 members, and they all seemed to pass us around.

A few weeks after the possible Nightstalker was on our roof, a couple from God's Own took me and my oldest brother, Hal, to their house for the day. I loved going to the Moore's house. It was huge and they had a shallow swimming pool I could walk in since I don't know how to swim. They had more grass in their yard than my entire neighborhood combined.

My mom had become very sporadic at that point. Mostly she was herself, the version that I loved and worried about. But she was slipping into that other version more frequently. My brothers had started acting odd too. Not exactly in the same way. It was more like they were leaving me out of things. They would all look at me, not blankly, more like they were angry. I felt like they were talking about me with Mom when I wasn't around. I felt like an outsider. When I was with others from God's Own, I didn't feel that way. I felt like I belonged.

That day changed things. Brother Moore was called away in the middle of the day. I'm not sure what his job was, but he got a phone call and left in a rush. Hal and I were in the backyard with Sister Moore. He and I were in the shallow pool and she was in a lawn chair next to the deeper pool. Once Brother Moore was gone, Sister Moore and Hal shared a look. I know I saw it. Very smoothly Hal grabbed me by the arms. I was ridiculously small and had no strength to resist. Sister Moore pulled a camera out of a small bag next to her chair. Hal lifted me out of the pool and then crouched down next to the pool. He held me on my stomach over his legs, my head facing away from Sister Moore. He grabbed the back of my shorts and pulled them down. I started screaming and wiggling. She started taking photos. They were both laughing. I kept trying to get away, but he was holding me tightly and he was so much bigger than me. I managed to grab the ledge of the pool and pulled myself out of his grip. I was probably only able to do that because we were both still wet and slick from the water.

  Hal looked angry. He started charging back into the pool. Sister Moore told him to stop. She said it was just a game and everything was done. He looked at her and nodded his head, then walked across the yard and into the house.

  I was still in the pool and realized I hadn't pulled my shorts back up. I grabbed them quickly and yanked them back into place. She just looked at me. Her large black sunglasses covered half of her face, so I couldn't see her eyes, but I could see her mouth. She was smiling at me.

  I didn't say anything to either of them the rest of the day. When Brother Moore got back, he drove Hal and me back home. After he left, Mom asked us both how the day was. I started crying and telling her what happened, but before I could even finish, she told me to stop tattling on my brother. He sat in a chair in the living room, arms crossed and smirking. I kept trying to tell her, thinking she just didn't understand what he and Sister Moore had done.

She screamed, "I told you to stop tattling on your brother! You never listen to me! You never listen to anyone! Go to your room, you're grounded! Don't you dare try to come out until I tell you to come out!"

At that point I just accepted that something in our family had changed and that I would be left permanently confused and disoriented. I ran to my room, still crying. My brother had stripped me naked, a grown woman who I had trusted took photos of me nude, they were laughing about it and called it a game, and then, my mom punished me for talking about it. I wanted to leave and never go back.

Five

Soon after that – by soon I mean a few weeks – Mom woke us up one Saturday morning and said we needed to have a family meeting. I was rather surprised, not that she wanted to have a family meeting, but that I was being included in it. I had started being cut out of more things. If I wasn't at school or with someone from God's Own, I was alone in my bedroom reading. My mom and brothers would all stay in the living room watching the news.

I could tell that whatever she had to say, it was going to be big. She was nervous. We didn't often hear her voice waver, but that time her voice was all over the place.

"I have a plan, but I'm only going to do it if each and every one of you agree. I think it's time we leave here. I want to move back to Iowa. My family is there and they are ready to accept us and help us. I know it's a huge change. You would each be leaving your school and your friends. You would be starting new somewhere you don't remember being before. That's why we won't do it unless you all agree."

Hal was the first to speak up.

"Why do we need to leave? Why can't we stay here?"

"I don't have a job. All I have is a high school diploma. I can't find work, and we are losing the house. The man we rent it from wants us out. I have enough money saved from the child support that social security gives me each month that I can buy us a used car. Either we can use that car to move to Iowa and get the help of my family, or we can stay here and live in the car until another opportunity presents itself."

She was very matter-of-fact about it all, but still had a nervous voice.

For my part, I jumped at the chance. I loved my friends and I loved California, but as soon as she brought this up, I was struck with hope that a fresh start would fix everything. The naivety of a child. One by one my brothers agreed as well.

"I'll think about timing and then let you know the final plan so you can let your friends know."

I had a feeling she already knew her 'final plan' and that even if any of us had dissented we would still be moving.

As we started to disperse, she held me behind in the kitchen. Family meetings were always held around the kitchen table. Once my brothers were gone, she started talking again. I was sitting to her right, but she wasn't looking at me. She was looking at the other end of the table.

"You can stay here. I'm not going to make you stay. The Moore's have offered to adopt you, but they said you have to be willing. If you want, I'll let them. You can stay here with your friends and the rest of us will move. You have to make your decision right now. If you want to stay, they'll pick you up this evening. You'll have your own bedroom and lots of books. You know they have money. They can give you a life I won't."

It was all said in a flat affect. No emotion, no nerves. Looking back, I know she wanted me to stay. She wanted me out of the family. I just didn't realize it at the time. I thought she was staying emotionless because she would be so hurt if I said yes and wanted to stay. Just weeks earlier I would have done anything to get away from my family, but a boy's emotions are fickle.

"No! I love you! I want to go! Please don't make me stay

here!"

I didn't cry, but I was close.

"Fine, you'll come with us. I'll let them know. But know it isn't going to be easy. And you have to make changes."

Then she stood up, grabbed the phone from the wall and walked into Hal and Grady's bedroom. I didn't hear anything from the room, but I think she must have called the Moore's to tell them my decision. I had no idea what changes she was talking about. I always tried to be good, always tried to do what I could to keep the other version of her from coming out.

Six

We left the first week of June in 1987. Mom had bought a '76 yellow Dodge Aspen. She rented a U-Haul trailer and we spent a week packing. The U-Haul was small, so we didn't take any furniture. It was filled mostly with clothes and Mom's collection of books God's Own had printed. They were thick like encyclopedias and there were dozens and dozens of them. Mostly they were bound volumes of shorter works. Others were on specific topics, like Armageddon, the evils of gay people, and how to convert Worldly people as long as they weren't gay.

The car didn't have working air, and as miserable as the heat was in our part of California in June, it was nothing compared to the heat in Death Valley. It didn't help that the only food Mom brought for the entire trip was peanut butter and jelly sandwiches. Our only fluids came from rest stop water fountains. Some nights we slept in the car, some nights she was able to get a cheap hotel room and we would all pile in. I don't recall much about the trip itself, other than my younger brother, Jeremiah, and I sitting in the front passenger seat together when he threw up all over our feet. We were still in Death Valley, the heat was brutal, and he barfed peanut butter all over my legs and shoes. The car reeked of it the rest of the trip.

I'm not sure how long the trip should have taken, but it took us about a week and a half. Driving across country with four boys was not a great situation. The intolerable *are we there yet?* was obviously fraying Mom which led to frequent stops. Not to mention the one song Hal and Grady played on repeat the entire trip.

The night we arrived at our destination we found out Mom had lied to us. The core point of the trip was to reunite with her family, then they would help us get established in our new lives. The entire trip she told us that was the plan, that as soon as we arrived, we would go to her sister's house and stay with her family until Mom had a job and we had a place of our own. It was nighttime when we got to Meribald and instead of taking us to her sister's house, she pulled over on the side of a dirt road. Hal asked her why she'd stopped the car and things came spilling out of her.

"My family doesn't know we're here. I didn't talk to them. They aren't going to help us. No one is going to help us. We have to do this on our own."

There we were, on a dirt road in Meribald, Iowa. All we had to our name was clothes, books, and a quickly dwindling amount of peanut butter and jelly.

We moved from road to road, but for about a month we were homeless living out of that car. I guess someone noticed eventually and contacted the police. They found us one evening and started talking to Mom. I heard bits and pieces of what she told them, that she was a poor single mother whose family abandoned her and she had no job or money and now we were all homeless. They took us to the local hotel and worked out an agreement with the owner. The police department had a special fund they could use to help us.

Our room was sort of like an efficiency apartment. There was a large bed, then in a corner of the room there was a kitchen. The bathroom was off the kitchen. The police came back daily to check on us. Most of the time they brought us groceries too. They would play with us out in the parking lot. One day they even brought us used bikes, but there were only three so I didn't get one. They helped Mom find a job at a local factory. They helped her find the trailer one town away that we moved into. It was a bit of a whirlwind. I think the trip was about a week and a half, we lived out of the car for about a month, then we lived in the hotel for about a month. By the time we moved to the trailer it was nearly time to start school again.

After we settled into the trailer in Lankon, but before we started school, she connected with the local congregation of God's Own. The first meeting we went to was a Thursday evening. I was excited. I thought it was how we were going to make friends. I wanted to feel their acceptance again. Instead, it was unrecognizable. There were around a hundred people there, mostly families, but they all looked so stern. They were talking quietly to each other before the meeting started, but it wasn't jovial like in our old congregation. During a meeting there are talks—that's what God's Own calls their version of sermons. On Thursdays, each talk was roughly five minutes and the overall meeting was two hours. Not just the overseer or drudges gave the talks, the brothers did as well. The sisters weren't allowed to give talks. At least half of the talks were about how being gay is a choice people make and that God condemns it. The rest focused on the need to avoid speaking to Worldly people. It was like this congregation was an extreme version of the one from California. They took the same basic concepts but amplified them a hundredfold. They all seemed so angry.

Afterwards, our family had to meet with the overseer and a small group of the drudges. They told us that they checked on Mom's membership to God's Own and received her records from the congregation in California. I didn't even know they kept records. They told us that in order to remain members we needed to follow all of God's rules for us. They started lining out what those rules were: no birthdays or holidays; no associating with Worldly people in any way; when we started school we wouldn't be allowed to speak to teachers or classmates—we had to listen and do our homework, but we were not allowed to open our mouths to anyone who wasn't part of the congregation; we would have to report any member of the congregation we saw breaking any of the rules; we had to go to the meetings on Sunday, Wednesday, and Friday, then had to volunteer our time on Saturdays to clean and maintain the congregation building. The list just went on and on.

None of it sounded right, especially not being able to speak with anyone who wasn't a member. I knew there were Worldly people who were still good people. I didn't know what school was going to be like in Iowa, but in California my teachers were fantastic and I loved my friends even though they weren't part of God's Own. What we were being told just didn't feel right.

Mom ate it up. She was so overjoyed I thought she was going to start crying right there. These people hadn't lifted one finger to help us, and she was willing to sacrifice any normalcy we could have in a new life in order to please them. She had just found a group of people who would encourage the worst of her changing personality instead of identifying and treating it as a mental illness.

Seven

In the weeks before school started, Mom created a routine for us all. Monday through Friday she worked from seven a.m. to three-thirty p.m. She would get us up at four-thirty a.m. and we would all sit at the kitchen table. We had ten minutes for breakfast, cold cereal with milk so skim it was basically water. I'm pretty sure that once the milk container got halfway down, she refilled it with water to make it last longer. Once we finished breakfast, we had to pull out each of our copies of the *Reader's Calendar*. It was a book created by God's Own. It was 365 pages. Each page was a day of the year. For each day there was a verse of the bible. These weren't in any particular order. One day it might be a verse from Revelations, the next day might be from Judges. After the verse there would be a few paragraphs explaining God's Own interpretation of the verse. Even before reading the interpretation, I could tell what it would say. All I had to do was think of the most extreme, intolerant, and punitive version of what the verse could mean, and that's what the interpretation would be.

It was a random realization, but it was during one of these morning *Reader's Calendar* sessions that I realized there was no diversity in the local congregation. Everyone was white. In California our congregation was a mix of nearly every race I'd heard of at that point in my life.

The *Reader's Calendar* took around twenty minutes for us to read and then discuss, so it was usually around five a.m. when we finished, but that didn't mean we were done. Each month

God's Own put out a large newspaper called The News. Each issue had many articles. Once we were done with the reader's calendar, Mom would hand out our copies of The News and we had to read an article she chose and discuss each paragraph. We did a round table type of thing. One of us would read the first paragraph, Mom would ask the associated questions that were printed on the back page, the one of us who had read the paragraph had to answer the questions. Then the next one would read the next paragraph, and the whole thing would continue. This usually took around an hour. By then it was roughly six a.m. and Mom would start getting ready for work. At that point we didn't have to stay at the kitchen table, but we did have to read *the bible*. She didn't give us specific books, chapters, or verses to read, but she expected us to highlight and annotate the parts we either felt were important or that we had questions about.

When she got home from work, she would sit us down in the living room. We had a couch and one chair. Mom would sit in the middle of the couch with Hal and Grady on either side. Jeremiah would sit in the chair. I had to sit on the floor. We then had to discuss what each of us had read in *the bible* that day, discuss what was important and what we had questions about. I always took the longest because I was a quick and comprehensive reader. I was only nine years old, but I always had a solid logic and comprehension level for what I would read. My brothers' questions were always basic: How big were the Nephilim? Did Samson really rip a lion apart with his bare hands? Why didn't anyone kill Jezebel sooner?

Mine were deeper. I knew she wouldn't be able to answer most of my questions, so I'd keep a list of them that I thought I'd need to ask the overseer instead. I would always give great detail regarding what I'd read, and I did ask Mom some questions, more wanting her opinion than a hard answer. One of my questions for her was about why we couldn't celebrate birthdays. I knew God's Own view on it, they said that there were only two birthday parties mentioned in *the bible* and that at each of those birthday parties someone had their head chopped off. God's Own interpreted this to mean that birthday parties were bad because they were bringing glory to a human instead of to God and his son, and that because of that, birthday parties led to death. This was an extremely illogical jump in my opinion as I could find nowhere in *the bible* that directly condemned birthdays. I thought for sure I was missing something and that there must have been more information to inform that interpretation.

When my brothers would ask their questions, Mom had kind answers for them. Again, they weren't particularly tough questions and so they probably made her feel like an expert when she was able to answer them. I don't think she understood that when I asked my questions, I didn't want some theological well thought out answer, I just wanted her opinion. I wanted to know why she personally agreed with every single interpretation given by God's Own. Her response to me over and over was that I needed to have faith, that asking questions like that meant that I wasn't showing faith and I'd be punished by God if I kept it up.

It took time, but eventually between these sessions and the content delivered during the meetings, I realized that members of God's Own weren't allowed to have opinions. God's Own interpreted every verse of *the bible* and we had to accept what they provided as absolute fact. Dissension, even asking questions that sounded like they might be based in disagreement, was punishable. We could only ask questions if they were worded in a way that gave the impression we were seeking to learn and understand instead of seeking to contradict.

You'd think that even if we could not have an opinion on matters of *the bible*, that we could have opinions outside of that. We couldn't. As members we were expected to live our entire life around t*he bible* and the teachings of God's Own. Discussing anything that wasn't *bible* related was a sin. Not living every second of our life to bring glory to God was a sin.

After we debriefed what we'd each read in the bible that day, I would go to my room and read one of the books I'd checked out from the library. I was surprised I was still allowed to do that, given they were fiction books and not religious books supplied by God's Own. I again shared a room with my younger brother. It was the smaller of the two bedrooms in the single-wide trailer. Mom had Hal and Grady sleep in the living room on a pull out couch and she took the larger bedroom to herself. When I'd go read, the rest of them would sit in the living room, watching the news.

Dinner was always ready by five. Every night we sat around the kitchen table to eat. Before we could eat, we had to pray. We each had our assigned seats at the table: Mom at the head, Hal and Grady on the side to her left, Jeremiah and I at the side to her right. She would choose one of us each night to say the prayer. During dinner Mom would allow two types of conversation, either what was being reported on the news, or *the bible*.

After dinner I'd go back to my room and read. The rest of them would sit in the living room and talk or watch more local news, or news specials if they were on.

Prior to bed we had to come together again and re-review the article we had read in the morning. Then she would assign us which article we would be reading the next morning. When it was bedtime, she would come to our beds one by one and we'd have to pray out loud while she listened. I was always last. The next day we'd go through the same process again. The only differences were on Wednesday and Friday evenings. We attended the meetings at the congregation those evenings.

Weekends were more intense, though we did get to sleep in a bit on Saturday. Also, she never actually made us volunteer the time to the congregation maintenance that we were supposed to do. She probably told them what she was having us do instead, and they thought it was a better use of our time. On Saturdays she'd get us up by seven. We'd get a ten-minute cold cereal breakfast, then we would spend four hours reading and discussing one of God's Own book publications, those special topics I mentioned before. Her favorite was one titled *The End Times and You*. It was a blow-by-blow of the book of Revelations. As I'm sure anyone would expect, God's Own's interpretation of the book was a literal one. Mom had become a sucker for fire and brimstone tactics. She equally loved hearing and saying them.

We'd have a short break for lunch, usually plain bologna sandwiches. After lunch we had to make reports. For this she would give us each a section of the newspaper. We had to read our section and write a report that identified why the people being reported on were evil, why they deserved the horrible things that had happened to them, why they deserved to die under God's wrath, and so on. We had five hours to complete it and we had to provide *bible* references and quotes fully annotated. At the end of the five hours we would have dinner. As soon as dinner ended, we each had to read our reports out loud. We went to bed early on Saturdays.

Sunday mornings we would get up at four a.m. have a quick breakfast, get cleaned up and changed, and drive to the congregation. The building was only about twenty-five minutes from our trailer and the meeting didn't start until nine-thirty a.m. but she would get us there around five a.m. It wasn't like a church where it's often left unlocked and you could just go in. We had to sit in the car in the parking lot until the overseer or one of the drudges got there and unlocked the building, usually around nine a.m. During the time sitting in the car, we weren't allowed to talk. She wanted us to ready ourselves for the great bounty of knowledge we would receive during the morning meeting. I didn't understand why we had to get there so early, but I guess it was just my mom wanting to make a show that she and her children were always the first to be there and ready for service. The Sunday meeting was supposed to end at eleven-thirty a.m. but the drudge who would give the final prayer before dismissal was extremely long winded. He would drone on and on for upwards of twenty to thirty minutes with us all standing there, eyes closed, heads bowed, hands clasped. Often it was noon before he finished.

Afterward we would go home, have a quick lunch, usually leftovers from dinner the night before. Then we would spend the entire afternoon and evening recapping everything we had read in the various material, everything we'd listened to during the meetings, and everything we'd reported on from the previous week.

There was truly little change when we started school. Mornings, evenings, and weekends stayed the same. We were expected to continue with our *bible* reading at school during breaks and on the bus ride to and from school. While at school we were not allowed to speak. The basic rule was that we were only allowed to open our mouths if we were in the trailer or with the congregation. Every morning before we'd go to school, she would tell us to watch each other, and that if any of us saw another one of us speaking with anyone we had to tell her as soon as she got home. This was an expectation God's Own had too. During a meeting, usually the Sunday meeting, they would remind all the school age children of the rules and say that we had to report directly to the overseer if we saw any of our peers in the congregation break any of the rules.

Eight

Mom didn't seem to care whether we did our homework or not. She didn't build time for that into our schedules. She had expectations that we all receive passing grades since we represented God's Own, but we were on our own in figuring out how to do that when every minute of our day outside of the classroom was spent on *the bible*.

Still wanting Mom to accept and love me, I tried as hard as I could to excel at my studies in school. She didn't know, but I had a flashlight under my mattress and after everyone went to bed and I could hear her snoring from the other end of the trailer I'd go under my blankets, turn on my flashlight, and do my homework. I would usually finish around midnight.

In California I was on the honor roll every quarter. To get on honor roll you could get one B, but the rest of your grades had to be A's. From 1st grade to 4th, I was a straight A student. Getting on honor roll was great because at the end of the quarter they would take us on a field trip to Las Angeles where we'd go to a small old theater that only showed classic black and white monster movies. I loved it. Of course that was when I was still allowed to speak to people.

Iowa school was different. Between Mom's new religious zealousness, the move, losing my friends, and not being able to speak with anyone, my grades suffered. My first year in Iowa was the fifth grade. I got mostly Bs and a few Cs that first quarter. My brothers got mostly Ds and Fs. When we brought home our report cards for that first quarter, she had each of us come sit at the kitchen table with her one at a time. We knew each other's grades before Mom did, so I wasn't worried since I'd received the highest grades of the four of us. She met with Hal first. He had the worst grades. Mostly Fs with a few Ds. He'd also skipped school a lot. I really thought Mom would lose it on him. Instead, she tried to bargain with him. She said that if he could bring his grades up to Cs and Ds by the end of the second quarter, she'd buy him a BB gun.

Next, she met with Grady. It was a similar agreement. If he'd bring his grades up from primarily Ds to Cs, she'd buy him a video game system.

I thought I'd be next, but instead she called Jeremiah over. He was getting a few Cs and mostly Ds. She told him that if he would get rid of the Ds and get at least all Cs by the end of the next quarter she would get him a dog.

I was up last. I sat down in the chair next to her wondering what she would offer me. I was prepared to tell her she didn't need to get me anything, that I wanted to do better and make her proud. There was no bargaining. First, she told me that she was so disappointed in me that she was sick to her stomach. She asked me if I understood how much restraint it was taking on her part to not beat me to impress upon me how upset she was. She told me that I owed everything to God and that every grade lower than an A was a slap in his face. She said I should be ashamed of myself. I just sat there not speaking. It was all rhetorical. She wasn't looking for me to answer, she just wanted me to be disgusted with myself. She ended by telling me to go to my room because she couldn't stand to see my face any more. She didn't let me out the rest of the night. I didn't get to use the bathroom or eat dinner.

Nine

The second quarter of the school year droned on much like the first. I was better in school than my brothers, I was better with the congregation than my brothers, I was more respectful to my mom than my brothers, but she treated them like anointed saints and treated me like devil spawn. By that point, most of the time she refused to even look at me. She spoke to me even less. When she did speak to me it was just to make sure I knew I was a disappointment. There was no logic that I could identify. No matter what I did she made sure I knew that I was an awful person. I wouldn't have thought it possible, but just before my tenth birthday in early December, things got worse.

She and my brothers were watching the news one evening and I was reading in my bedroom. There was a story about starving Ethiopians. I didn't see it, but I could certainly hear it. Once the story was over, I heard a shuffling in the doorway to my room. I looked up from my book and saw my mom standing in the doorway. It was that look again. The one where she was looking into or through me.

"I want you to tell me why," she said in the flat voice, the terrifying voice. Though she had threatened me with it, she hadn't actually hit me since the playground. Don't get me wrong, she'd spanked me, but when she did, she wasn't out of control. It was the normal kind of spanking some children get, more embarrassing than painful. But when she talked like this, I knew her anger was tethered by a fraying string.

"I'm not sure what you're talking about."

My mind raced. I retraced the week trying to figure out if I'd done or said something sinful. Or had one of my brothers told her something about me that wasn't true? They had taken to doing that. It was misdirection. They would skip school or not do their *bible* readings, and before Mom could get mad at them, they would say something false about me, knowing that her anger toward me would blind her to anything they had done. It's why I pretty much lived in my bedroom at that point.

"You're killing them. We both know you're doing it. All of those Ethiopians. I want you... to tell me... right now... why... you're doing this... to them."

She paused every few words. That was new. Still the blank look through me.

As usual, I tried to approach it rationally. I should have just accepted her blame and apologized.

"I-I'm here, I'm not in Ethiopia. I'm not doing anything to them."

At that point I was starting to stutter and speak slowly. I tried to consider every word deliberately.

I was sitting on my bed which was just across from the doorway. I was at the head of the bed next to the wall. In a flash she was in front of me. She backhanded the right side of my face so hard that the left side of my head slammed into the wall. Things spun for a few seconds and my eyes watered. The hit stung my skin, but most of my head just felt numb. I wasn't even sure what had just happened.

She didn't say anything. She was just gone from the room and I was left there alone feeling like I was going to vomit. I couldn't believe that was my life. I was sure God was punishing me, I just wasn't sure what I had done to deserve it.

I stayed there, stunned, for some time. After a while my younger brother came to the door.

"Mom said to get to the table now. It's dinner, and you're saying the prayer."

He smugly smiled the entire time. I wanted to hit him.

I went to the table without saying a word. I sat down in my normal spot. She looked at me and said," Say the prayer, and you better mean it." Her voice was venom.

I bowed my head, shut my eyes, and clasped my hands.

"Dear God, please accept our humble thanks for the food you have provided us. Thank you for the congregation. Thank you for our family. Thank you for all the guidance you provide us. We thank you for all this in the name of your son, Jesus Christ. Amen."

My voice shook the entire time. I opened my eyes and all four of them were staring at me. Mom was shaking.

"You're killing them! You… are… killing them all, and you think that's fine? You think you don't even need to pray for them? Do it again. And do it right!"

All three of my brothers smirked and giggled. I don't know if Mom was so focused on me that she didn't realize it was all a joke to them, or if she just didn't care.

"Dear God, please help the starving Ethiopians. We have a bounty and they have none. We ask you for this, in the name of your dear son Jesus Christ. Amen."

My face still stung where she hit me. My eyes were watering.

Her palms slammed on the table. It felt like the whole room shook. The giggles stopped.

"Go to your room until you're ready to take this seriously!"

I didn't hesitate. In one motion I pushed my chair back and ran to my bedroom. I was shaking so hard it hurt. I fell asleep crying in my pillow while they laughed in the kitchen.

I woke up around one in the morning. The Dark Woman was at the foot of my bed. This was the first time she did more than just stand there. She turned her head toward the window and pointed outside. I looked out the window but there was nothing there, just a giant corn field across the street from the trailer park. I looked back toward her, but she was gone.

Ten

My tenth birthday came in early December. Since we didn't celebrate birthdays, I didn't even realize it. When Mom got home from work, I was in my bedroom just sitting on the bed. I wasn't reading. I was tense all the time. I tried to not even move. I thought that if I just didn't do anything then no one could get mad at me. No one could blame me for anything. My brothers were all in the living room, talking and laughing. They always seemed to be talking and laughing. I'm sure it was about me. It was always about me.

Mom called me into the kitchen. She stood in front of the refrigerator with her hands on her hips.

"Now that you're ten, I'm adding another chore to your list. It's time you start doing more to help out around here."

She kept a list on the refrigerator. It had each of our names side by side and listed the chores we were responsible for underneath.

Hal (twelve): Set alarm clock each night before bed.
Grady (eleven): Watch the news for school cancellations in winter.
Jeremiah (eight): Take a bath twice a week.
Hezekiah (nine): Sweep and mop the kitchen, hall, and bathroom. Scrub the toilet and bathtub. Vacuum the living room and bedrooms. Dust everywhere. Clean the fireplace. Bring wood in from the shed. Wash the dishes. Scrub the stove and sink.

She scrubbed off the (nine) next to my name and changed it to (ten). She added *Get the mail daily* to the end of my list.

"You start tomorrow."

I hadn't noticed earlier, but Jeremiah was then standing next to me, looking at the list on the refrigerator. He didn't speak to me often, so I was a little surprised when he reached out to shake my hand. Without thinking, I took his hand.

"I didn't even know you turned ten today. Congratulations!"

I didn't respond. It was such an unusual thing to say. I think I cocked an eyebrow and just looked at him.

Mom responded. She responded by grabbing me by both arms and lifting me off the ground. I screamed in surprise. As usual I had no idea what was going on. She looked so angry. She threw me stomach first over the back of the large chair in the living room. Before I knew what was going on she had pulled down my pants and started spanking me. I don't remember exactly what she was yelling, but it was something about knowing better than to celebrate my birthday.

There was no logic to it. I hadn't celebrated anything. At most, Jeremiah was the one who congratulated me for being ten. This wasn't a normal spanking. It hurt so much my legs were going numb. It just kept going. It wasn't a few slaps and then done, it just went on and on, and she was hitting so hard. My brothers were laughing. They were laughing about seeing my naked butt. They were talking about how red it and my legs were getting. They thought it was all so funny.

When she was done, she just let go of me and let me fall to the ground. I tried to pull up my pants but I was crumpled on the ground and it hurt so much. I managed to get them up and crawled on my hands and knees to my bedroom. Mom just stood there, huffing from the exertion. My brothers were still laughing and talking about me being a dramatic crybaby, crawling on the ground. I wasn't being dramatic; she had hit my backside and legs so hard and so much I didn't think I could put weight on them.

I stayed under the covers of my bed just shaking until dinner. Ever since the starving Ethiopians news story, she had made me say every dinner prayer. It was scripted at that point. I had to thank God for everything he'd given us, thank him for a mother who cared enough to teach me what I was doing wrong, thank him for his direction, then I had to apologize for all the horrible things I was doing to the world. By my tenth birthday that list had grown to causing the Ethiopians to starve, starting any wildfire that happened in the country, increasing crime across the world, as well as any skirmish or war that was going on. Her view of me had gotten so out of hand that she really did believe I was an anti-Christ. It wasn't just a passing thing she said. She really did feel that I was the root of all evil in the world. She thought that I knew I was the root of all evil, and that I enjoyed causing others pain in service of my father, Satan.

Since I had to do the dinner prayer, I knew there was no way she would just leave me alone in my room. She came to get me herself that time.

"If you know what's good for you, you're going to do it right."

I was able to walk, slowly, to the table. I delivered the script as well as I could, ignoring the snickers from my brothers. By this point things had degraded when it came to the schedule we were supposed to keep, at least sort of. I was still expected to keep the rigid schedule built around studying and living *the bible* and the teachings of God's Own. My brothers weren't. The days of only being allowed to discuss *the bible* and the news at dinner were over. They talked about whatever they felt like. That dinner all they talked about were other things that were as red as my butt and legs after Mom spanked me. Mom just sat smug at the head of the table, so proud of herself. I knew that if I said anything in defense of myself, or said anything at all, I'd be screamed at, likely hit, and sent to bed with no food or water for the rest of the night. I just had to sit there and listen.

Everything I did was controlled. She would watch me. I had to chew every bite twenty times before I was allowed to swallow. If I didn't, it was a backhand. I had to ask her permission to take more food if I wanted seconds. If I didn't, it was a backhand. I had to ask her to be excused from the table. If I didn't, it was a backhand. It wasn't just at dinner either. If I had to use the bathroom, I had to ask her permission. She would make me tell her exactly what I needed to do in there. On the times she gave me permission she would set a small kitchen timer for either forty-five seconds or two minutes. If I wasn't done and out of the bathroom by the time the alarm went off, she would slam open the door with my brothers right at her side. No matter what I was doing, they would all just stand there watching me until I was done.

These requirements didn't apply to any of my brothers. They were free to come and go as they pleased. They had Worldly friends, they talked to people at school and out in public, they stayed at friends' houses overnight, they rarely went to the meetings any more. None of it seemed to register with Mom as being against God's Own rules. The rules only applied to me.

She spent less and less time with my brothers. By my birthday, a typical day consisted of her coming home from work and going straight to bed. She'd get up long enough to make sandwiches or spaghetti for dinner, we'd all eat, and she'd go back to bed again. She was always lethargic and only seemed to show any focus when she was angry with me.

Her attitude toward me had really started rubbing off on my brothers too, particularly Hal. We barely spoke, but he hit me even more often than Mom. It took no provocation with him. We'd get home from school, and he'd just deck me in the back of the head. I lost consciousness more than once. Or he'd pin me on the ground in the living room and just punch my side. A few times he'd pinned me down and twisted the skin on my arms and legs to see how long it would take to start bleeding.

Between Mom and Hal, I was always covered in bruises and cuts. I wore a lot of long-sleeved shirts and never wore shorts. I tried to cover everything.

I don't think Mom even knew what Hal was doing. I think he did it because he knew there was nothing I could do about it. If he'd been abusing Grady or Jeremiah, they would have been able to tell Mom and she would have done something about it. I couldn't tell her. If I had it would have worked out one of two ways. The most likely is that she wouldn't have believed me, and then she would have punished me for lying. Or, she would have believed me, but told me that I was evil and deserved it. Then she would have bought Hal a gift for showing initiative and having the courage to stand up to me.

Eleven

I'm going to change things up now and skip forward a few years. Just imagine the events I just wrote about going on daily during the time I'm skipping. I really don't want to bring up every little event that happened. It's hard enough having lived through it all. I don't want to have to dwell on every bit of it now. Just know that things didn't get better, they just kept getting worse. I'm going to skip to the next big event, which was in the summer break of 1992, so I had turned fourteen the previous December. I had just finished my last year of junior high. It had been miserable.

The year before, Hal had flunked his freshman year of high school. Straight Fs. Instead of repeating the grade, which would have then put him in the same grade as Grady, he dropped out. He told Mom he'd get a job and eventually take the equivalency test for his GED. By then he was a serious drug user, but all his connections were at school. Since he was no longer in school, he couldn't get his drugs as regularly as he would have liked. He was bad to me before, but the combination of being a total failure and not having a regular source for his drugs made him so much worse. I had no idea how much worse he could be.

I had a bad summer cold. It wouldn't go away, or even alleviate. Mom had planned a weekend trip to Springfield for a special assembly of God's Own. She decided to take Grady and Jeremiah with her. They begged to go so they could hang out at the hotel pool while she was at the assembly. She left me behind with Hal. It wasn't out of any sympathy for me. She just didn't want to catch my cold, so of course she didn't want to be trapped in a car with me for hours.

Mom, Grady, and Jeremiah left around noon on Friday. They were set to return Sunday evening. It was hot outside, but it was hotter inside. The trailer did have central air, but Mom wouldn't let us use it, it cost too much money. Instead, she had this method of opening the windows just a crack and putting sticks she'd cut to size in the window frames, preventing them from being opened further from the outside. All it would take was some jostling of the frame to knock the sticks loose, but she never realized that. She'd set some cheap box fans in each of the doorways in an attempt to create air circulation.

My plan for the weekend was to stay in bed and try to read my books. I hadn't really been able to read for a few weeks. It was too hard to concentrate when I was so sick. My sinuses were still clogged, my throat raw, and I had constant changes between body shaking chills and boiling temperatures, but the headache was becoming manageable. The headache was what had really kept me from concentrating.

They were gone about five minutes when Hal called my name.

"Hez! Come out here!"

He wasn't really yelling as much as he was just speaking loudly. I stayed in bed, pretending to be asleep.

"Hez! Hez! Hez! Heeeeeez!" He just kept on, over and over. I stayed in bed with my eyes closed.

He came to my room and opened the door. He stopped next to my bed and leaned his head down, right next to my ear.

"*Living room, now, you fucking dumbass!*"

Then he jerked the blankets off my bed, wrapped one arm

around me, and flipped me onto the floor. As I hit the floor, he was already walking back into the living room.

Something I haven't really mentioned was my physical stature. I was fourteen years old and Hal was sixteen or seventeen. I had just completed eighth grade. I was maybe eighty pounds. Each of my brothers were much more normal sized for their ages. Hal was basically the size of a lithe, grown man. Grady was always a little heavy. Jeremiah had been taller and weighed more than me for several years, even though I was just over a year older than him. I think it was my nerves that caused it. From the time we moved to Iowa, I was in constant tension. I was constantly fearful. I think the ongoing attack on my nerves led to my small stature.

By that point in time, I didn't cry. Sometimes I thought I would, but it really felt like I had used up all my tears. My body just refused to produce any more. My mom's abuse had grown a little less physical and more mental. She had stopped backhanding me, but she still spanked me. I think that was less about physically hurting me and more about humiliating me. She would always rip my pants down to do it, no matter who was around. It would happen at home, it would happen at the congregation, it would happen at the library, at the store, in the yard, anywhere she thought I'd wronged her or God. Most of the adults would act like they didn't see anything. The children would all laugh and point. I felt like the town joke.

Hal's abuse remained very physical. I don't think he was smart enough to employ mental abuse. He would try to at times, but he just didn't have the ability to hurt with words like Mom could. Or maybe it was because I still remembered loving my mom, but I couldn't remember that feeling for my brothers. I still remembered the fact that in California we were all close and cared for each other, but I couldn't remember the feeling the way I could with Mom.

I picked myself up off the floor, blew my nose, put a cough drop in my mouth, and walked out to the living room.

"I'm sick and I'm tired and I really just want to sleep. What do you need?"

I couldn't look at him. Eye contact would provoke him. As normal, I just looked at the floor in front of me. Even today I don't look up when I'm walking, I just look at the ground in front of me all the time. It's also still extremely difficult for me to make eye contact when I talk to someone. I'm always looking off to the side. Usually I carry a notebook with me and I'm always making notes. It's not because I need notes on everything, it just gives me something to look at instead of the people I'm talking to.

"God doesn't exist, Mom hates you, and you belong to me. You are my property. I can do whatever I want with you and no one will care. You could disappear and no one would care. No one likes seeing you. You're the worst kind of person. Take off your clothes and get on the floor."

He wasn't yelling, just deliberate. I could tell he'd planned this as a speech. He was trying to be ominous and intimidating. I looked in the middle of the room and there was a blanket spread out with a knife on the floor next to it.

"No, I'm going back to bed. Leave me alone. I don't want to get you sick."

I didn't have any idea what he was planning. I hoped the thought of getting him sick would deter him. Telling me to take my clothes off wasn't unusual. Me being naked while everyone else had on clothes was one of my mom's favorite humiliation techniques.

I wasn't thinking or moving quickly due to being sick and

exhausted. He was on me before I even turned around. I had just exhaled when he grabbed my throat with both his hands, so I had little to no air in my lungs. Both his thumbs dug into the soft part of my throat. It was just seconds before my eyes felt like they were bulging out of my head. I tried to claw at his hands and arms, but with my weak muscles it felt like pushing at steel. I started to see these specks of black outlined by bright light floating around everywhere, then those specks became longish splinters, then everything just kind of flashed and things started to spin. I passed out. When I woke up, I was face down on the floor in the middle of the blanket. I could tell I didn't have any clothes on. My legs were bent at the knees and my feet had been tied to my arms, which were pulled behind my back.

That was it. I knew I was going to die. I wasn't even upset. I was thankful it was all finally going to be over. I'd thought about suicide, a lot. I just couldn't do it. Maybe it was because I didn't know if God actually existed or not, and if he did it meant my life was a trial and suicide would not be the ending he was looking for. More likely, I'd been abused as long as I could remember and I just couldn't bring myself to hurt myself.

Death wasn't Hal's plan. I couldn't see him doing it, but I felt him slice into my skin. Shallow and short slices. As soon as he finished one, he started another.

Still, I didn't cry. I crushed my eyes shut as hard as I could. I tried to force myself out of my body, and so I did.

I wasn't floating over my body watching what was going on. My body didn't die when I left it, I just wasn't in it any more. I wasn't in the trailer any more. I was in that cracked earth place, the cat creature sitting directly in front of me. Momentarily I thought I had just passed out from the pain and was dreaming. I looked at myself and knew I wasn't dreaming. It's hard to explain, I could just tell. I was wearing a black suit, white shirt, black tie, and shiny black shoes. I had a silver watch on my left wrist; there was a fox head tie pin in the tie. I felt good. I felt strong. My head was clear.

I looked to my left and everything moved around me. I wasn't on the cracked earth with the cat any longer. I was on a tiny patch of land in the middle of a black, flat ocean. Small waves crashed at my feet. There was a noise behind me, and I turned around. I watched as hundreds of thick, green and yellow, tentacles breach the skin of the water. They didn't have suckers on them, but they did have large, sharp claws running their entire length. The noise sounded like a pod of whales all screaming at once. I looked in a different direction. Again everything moved past me in a blur.

I was in a dead forest. No leaves, no grass, just bare, dead trees clawing higher into the sky than I could see. I looked around but didn't see anything other than trees at first. I knew something had to be there. I felt it. The cracked earth had the cat creature, the black ocean had whatever connected the tentacles. This place had to have something. It made sense even though there was no one to explain any of it to me. I was just *getting* it.

Then I saw a small light in the distance. I walked toward it, it hovered toward me. I looked at my watch. I'd been walking toward it for fifteen minutes when we finally came face to face. It did have a face. A body too. It was a woman. She kind of looked like the Dark Woman, but she was muted by soft, glowing light. Her white dress was in tatters, like it had been ripped to shreds. Her long golden hair floated all around her, suspended in the air. She was young and beautiful. Her mouth was sealed shut. I looked closer. It looked like it had been sewn shut.

I pointed at her and said," I need you." She nodded her head and I was back in my body.

Hal was gone. I was still tied in the middle of the floor. There was blood all over the blanket. I saw the clock on the VCR. It was seven p.m. I'd been laying there for around seven hours. The pain, it was worse than anything I'd been through so far. My back, my legs, and my sides felt like they were on fire.

I didn't cry. I didn't whimper. I did start to shuffle, tried to loosen the ropes. Hal must have heard me. It's a weird thing, but what I remember very clearly were all the dust motes in the air. Just moving and swirling and twisting everywhere in a beam of light. They were all so clear. The pattern was beautiful, in a weird way.

Hal came out of the bathroom with some towels.

"Five thousand two hundred and ninety nine little cuts. One for every day we've had to suffer with you in our lives. You fucking asshole, you're disgusting."

Still tied up, he started wiping me down with the wet towels. He didn't talk any more, and neither did I. When he'd wiped up the blood from my skin, he opened a bottle of alcohol and poured it all over me. The burning was incredible. I still didn't cry. I just stayed in place, shaking. He grabbed a bunch of paper towels and pressed them all over me. He tried to tape them in place. He untied the ropes. My legs and arms crashed down to the floor. They were completely numb. I continued lying there.

"Go to bed, you fucking idiot."

The pain was severe and I couldn't feel my limbs, but I wouldn't crawl. It took time, but I got up and I walked, slowly. I stumbled to my bedroom and shut the door. I went to the dresser and pulled out a robe. After I wrapped it around myself, I got in bed face down and pulled the covers over me. I didn't sleep. I just waited.

Twelve

I didn't get out of bed the rest of the weekend. Twice a day Hal brought me a plain bologna sandwich and a glass of water. He'd also bring a few towels and a small bowl of water and hydrogen peroxide so I could clean my new wounds. Sunday morning, I used two small mirrors to examine what he'd done. I needed to know how bad it was—not that there was anything I could do about it. It still hurt and if I moved too much the slices would start bleeding again, but the damage didn't look as bad as I had imagined it would.

Sunday afternoon he came into my room.

"If you tell her, if you tell anyone, next time I'll kill you."

I believed him. I believed he would kill me, whether I told anyone or not.

Mom, Grady, and Jeremiah got back that evening. When I heard them parking, I forced myself onto my back for the first time since Friday. As soon as Jeremiah came into our room he started yelling about how bad it smelled. I hadn't even noticed. Mom came in, told me I was disgusting, then told me to go get a bath. Hal was behind her just staring at me. I'd been careful not to get any blood on my sheets when I was cleaning myself, so there was no trace. I did manage to get myself up and to the bathroom, but I was moving slowly and like a rickety old man. I'm sure Mom just thought it was from being sick for weeks with the never ending cold.

I stayed in the warm bath water as long as I could without

making it so long that Mom would come through the door, telling me I'd been taking too long. Once I was out and dried off, I looked through the cabinets. I found some ibuprofen and took a small handful with water from the sink. I didn't know whether it would help numb the pain, but it was worth a try. I dressed and went back to bed. None of the slices were visible. He'd kept them all on my legs and back, completely covered by my clothes.

I thought about the other places, the places when I pushed out of my body. I knew there were more than just the three I visited. I still didn't understand how I knew, but I did know. I also knew something else. I couldn't just push out of my body. I could push myself forward. Not in a physical time travel way, but I could push my mind forward. Ever since the playground in California I'd convinced myself it was just déjà vu, but I realized it wasn't. Once I was back in bed, that's what I did. I needed to know what was going to happen with the Glowing Woman.

It didn't take long. Within minutes I knew what was going to happen. I knew it would happen that night. I knew I wanted to see it in person. I needed to. I was resolved to it.

Mom gave me a small bowl of chicken noodle soup and a bologna sandwich for dinner. Before bed she even made me a glass of hot tea. It was mint. She hadn't done something like that for me since we lived in California. I think she knew something had happened that weekend. I don't think she knew exactly what, or how bad it was. I think she knew something was off and it confused her. Maybe she still had some maternal instincts that kicked in. I don't really know, but I was thankful for the tea.

Everyone went to bed and fell asleep, except for Hal and me. Before Jeremiah came to bed, I quietly got dressed in dark clothes then got back in bed and made sure I was completely covered by the blankets. Our bedroom door was open so I could see the foldout shared by Hal and Grady. I waited. I knew it wouldn't take long. Hal crept off the bed, careful not to shake it and wake Grady. He was in shorts and a t-shirt, but he had a bag of clothes waiting for him outside. He kept it stashed next to the shed. He'd been sneaking out for months, I just hadn't known where he was going when he did.

He quietly walked over to the window in the kitchen, removed the protective stick Mom had in place, lifted the window, pushed out the loose screen, and slipped out. It was a five-foot drop which he made with ease. I waited. After a few minutes, I followed. I didn't need to keep him in sight. I knew exactly where he was going. I was slow going and walked like a rickety old man again, but I knew the pain would be worth it.

Next to the trailer park there was a giant cow pasture. It was surrounded by an electric fence. I knew it was active because Hal pushed me against it every chance he got. In the front center area of the field, there was an abandoned schoolhouse. It was brick, two stories, and all the windows had been broken out by teenagers throwing rocks at them. I'd never been inside – that would be trespassing – but I'd heard that others hung out there and that the inside was full of graffiti. I waited at the edge of the field until I was sure Hal was inside. I crept under the fence and made my way to the building. I found a low window and dragged myself through. I quickly found the hallway I'd seen earlier. I crouched down, and I waited.

After a few minutes, Hal came into the large room connected to the hallway I was in. It was dark and he couldn't see me. He was using a very faint flashlight; it barely lit the immediate area around him. Its beam wouldn't be able to reach me even if he held it in my direction. There were cobwebs everywhere, rats scurried, something ran across my hand pressed to the ground. I should have been terrified. Instead I was excited. After that night he wouldn't be able to do anything to me again. My heart raced. It's the first time I remember smiling. I'm sure I looked crazy with my wide open eyes. I didn't want to blink; I didn't want to miss any of it. I deserved to see every second of what was going to happen.

He settled into a corner and pulled out a small cooler from his duffle bag. Suddenly, I shuddered. I thought I was going to collapse. The shudder felt like it had ripped open every slice, but it hadn't. I focused; I focused on why I was there. The more I focused, the stronger I felt. Not as strong as I felt in the other place, in my black suit, but strong enough.

Out of his cooler he pulled a six pack, obviously beer. Probably the cheapest thing he could convince an adult to buy for him. Or, more likely, he'd broken into someone else's trailer and stolen it. He downed three of them as I looked on from the hallway. He wasn't doing anything else, just drinking. He had this opportunity to do whatever he wanted. He didn't know I was there, he thought he was alone. He could have been reading, playing games, hanging out with friends, doing drugs, anything at all. He chose to sit in a corner of an abandoned building and drink. He was pathetic. The more I looked, the more my hate swelled.

He was starting on his fourth can when it happened. My spot was ideal. I could see the entire large room he was in. I saw the light begin to pour in. She came from the same doorway he had entered from. There were only two ways out, that doorway and the hallway I was in. He'd never reach either. It took him a few seconds longer than me to notice her. I don't know if he was already drunk, or just heavily buzzed, but he didn't move. It was his turn to be confused and disoriented. She continued to move toward him, hovering about a foot off the ground, toes pointing to the floor, tattered dress flittering around her, hair suspended all around like she was floating through water. I was far enough away that I couldn't be sure, but I think she flicked her eyes in my direction, making sure I was there to witness.

Hal yelled. It didn't sound like fear. More like he was trying to be intimidating. There was this light bathed woman floating in front of him, mouth sewn closed, and he thought he could scare her. She was feet away from him at that point and he still just sat on the ground with a beer in his hand. He really didn't look scared at all, just annoyed and angry. He lifted the beer to his mouth while her mouth started writhing. She reached up with her hands and used her jagged, bright, nails to rip at the threads that sealed it. As soon as they had all been ripped out, she distended her jaw and sucked in a huge breath of air. When she released it, she screamed. The scream was so loud the walls shook. I was on my hands and knees and the vibration she released caused me to fall flat on my face. As quickly as possible I looked back up. I couldn't miss what was going to happen. I needed to see, I needed to be sure. Her scream continued, focused directly on Hal. The beer in his hand had exploded, as well as the two full ones still on the ground next to him. She was so close to him at that point that I could see him very clearly. Her light encompassed him and the surrounding area. His jaw was dropped, he must have been screaming, but all I could hear was her. Her hair and dress swirled rapidly all around her. I looked back at Hal. There was blood. It streamed from his eyes, ears, nose, and mouth.

I kept watching. I held my hands over my ears. I knew there was nothing he could do to me and I knew she wouldn't hurt me, so I stood and walked into the room. Walking through her vibrations felt like walking through water. Not easy, but not impossible. I didn't get too close, but I wanted a better look. I wanted a front row seat.

I was maybe ten feet away when his head exploded. The same second his head burst, her scream stopped. Her light seemed to dim a bit. I hadn't noticed it at first, but her light had grown stronger the longer and louder she screamed. Her hair and dress began to settle, still suspended in the air, but swirling less.

She lifted a hand toward what was left of him and that hand began to glow. It got brighter and brighter until I had to cover my eyes and turn my head away. When I looked back, she was still there, but Hal's body and everything he'd brought were gone. I didn't know if she'd sent them somewhere else, or if she'd burned them from existence.

She was hovering, eyes on me. Again, I don't know how, but I knew what to do. I said clearly, "Thank you, you can go back now."

Then she was gone. Like the Dark Woman, there was no flash, no fading, no noise, nothing like that. She was there, and then she was gone.

I didn't have a watch, but I knew I needed to rush. I needed to get back to the trailer and back in bed. It was harder to pull myself up through the window than I thought it would be. In general, I underestimated how physically weak I was. It was made more difficult by the fact that I needed to keep from making any noise. I'm not sure how I did it, but I did. I got myself up and then started to reset the window screen. I realized before I was finished that I needed to leave it open. If everything was sealed up and Hal was gone, it would prompt questions. If the window was left open and the screen popped out, maybe they'd just think he ran away. I had enough wits about me that I grabbed a hand towel hanging from the stove and wiped down the windowsill. I knew it would take away Hal's fingerprints as well, but I didn't have a choice. I needed to make sure no one could find mine overlaying his if someone looked.

Given my complete inexperience and general frayed nerves, I still don't know how I pulled it off. I was able to wipe down the window, sneak past Grady, get back into the bedroom with Jeremiah, change clothes, and get back into bed, all without waking anyone.

My adrenaline was running hard. I was ecstatic. The joy I felt, the joy of getting revenge, the joy of knowing I had real power, the joy of knowing I had the power to change my life—it was unbelievable. I thought I wouldn't be able to sleep the rest of the night. Instead, I crashed almost immediately.

Thirteen

Mom was gone for work the next morning before I got up. While I was sick, she hadn't required me to get up for the *Reader's Calendar* or readings. Again, it wasn't out of kindness or pity. She just wanted to spend as little time around me as possible, so she wouldn't get sick. Either she had not noticed the kitchen window wide open and that Hal wasn't sleeping in the living room, or she just didn't care. I knew he had been sneaking out, so she probably did too. Grady and Jeremiah were still sleeping when I got up. I walked quietly to the bathroom so I could check for blood and clean anything I needed to before they woke up. After the exertion it took to get to the abandoned school, I figured I'd ripped open at least one of my wounds.

After I finished, I came back down the hall toward the kitchen. Grady was standing at the window, putting the screen back in. In case Mom hadn't seen it, he was making sure it was all reset before she'd have a chance to. Grady was Hal's extremely lazy lacky. He'd try to cover for him, try to hide any evidence of his drugs and alcohol.

With Mom at work and Hal gone, the day was uneventful. Grady and Jeremiah were always there to point, laugh, and contribute in whatever way they could when Mom or Hal were going at me, but they didn't really initiate things on their own.

I don't know if it was the relief from knowing that one of the largest contributors to my horrible, pathetic, life was gone, or if it just coincided with an improvement, but my cold really cleared up that day. Even the pain from Friday seemed to become tolerable. It got me wondering if it was another ability I had. I could go to the other places, push my mind forward to see things before they happened. Was there something that would let me heal quicker too? I seemed to understand instinctively some of what I could do, but I didn't fully understand it. The library had an occult section I'd never been in before. I thought that would be a good place to investigate, but I really had no way to get there.

Of course, now I know that I don't have healing powers. I can, however, visit one of the other places and bring a healer to mend me. He kind of looks like a frog sitting cross-legged, but he's gold and roughly the size of a two-story house, so I have to be careful to make sure there's plenty of open space when I bring him. He lives in a cave atop a mountain that's covered in snow. Not normal snow. On his mountain snowflakes are either yellow or blue. When they join on the ground, they turn green. It's beautiful to watch. He doesn't speak, none of them speak, but sometimes I visit him just to watch the snow.

I was feeling well enough that I decided to walk the few miles to get the mail that afternoon. I knew it would be slow going, but I felt so happy and confident with myself that I wanted to get out of the trailer. It's like I got that tiny shot of confidence, and suddenly everything looked different. I didn't walk on eggshells around Grady and Jeremiah. The sky looked bluer. The horizon looked brighter. I even smelled things I didn't remember smelling before. I walked out of the front of the trailer park. On the same side of the road, but to the right, was the cow pasture with the old school in it. I couldn't help it; I laughed when I saw it. Not a little, private, laugh. Loud, and long. Every laugh seemed to shoot another wave of relief over me, like shackles dropping off.

On the other side of the road was the giant open corn field, the one the Dark Woman had pointed to. I didn't know anything about farming, or crops, but that field always seemed to have corn in it at some varying stage from March to November. I smelled the earth. It smelled wonderful. It was so deep, it reminded me of freshly ground coffee. I had always wanted to try coffee, but Mom wouldn't allow it. All we had to drink was tap water and iced tea. The iced tea was really for Mom. She didn't like the idea of us having caffeine, so we only got a glass every week or two.

We'd each been getting a small allowance for the past few years. Hal was getting twenty dollars a month, Grady was getting fifteen, Jeremiah was getting ten, I was getting one. It didn't come out of Mom's paycheck. Since our dad wasn't in the picture and didn't pay child support, our mom said she received fifteen dollars a month for each of us. I think she said it was from social security, but I can't remember for sure. I was basically a captive, only allowed to leave home for school or to get the mail. Anywhere else and I was with Mom, who wouldn't let me buy anything. Since I hadn't spent any, it meant I had around twenty-five dollars in my wallet.

On the way to the post office there was a small convenience store. I had never been inside since Mom only shopped at one grocery store a town over. I decided to check it out. They rented videotapes that were kept along a back wall. There were five or so aisles in the place. Most of the aisles had light groceries. One was lined with candy, chips, and sodas. That was not what I was looking for though. I walked to the far end of the counter, where I saw the coffee. It was nothing fancy, just a few drip pots, some sugar in a jar, and some milk in a pitcher. I filled a to go cup, added a few shakes of sugar, and about three tablespoons of milk.

It cost thirty-five cents.

I stepped outside, looked out at the cornfield across the street, and genuinely enjoyed my very first sip of coffee. I decided to go get the mail, I decided to get coffee, I had money to pay for it. I was in control. I loved the way that felt. It was a rush I'd never experienced, making decisions for myself. I'd heard about free will before, God's Own talked about it all the time, but I'd never experienced it. Not like I did in that moment.

The field intrigued me. It was so large, and the corn obstructed the view of anything that might be in the distance. It seemed like a perfect area for a few tests.

From the convenience store, I turned right. It was another two blocks, just past the railroad tracks, to the white-bricked post office. It was one of those post offices you might see in old movies. First off, it was small. About the size of an average living room. The part you'd walk into with all the mailboxes was only about a quarter of the place. The rest was hidden behind the boxes and the front desk. The wall with the front desk was bricked, with a window-sized opening which was barred. When you got stamps, you'd have to slide your money under the bars, and the woman who worked there would slide your stamps back under. If you got a package, you had to walk outside. The woman would come out of her cage and put your package on the floor of the lobby area. She'd tap on a window when she was back in her cage, letting you know it was OK for you to come back inside and grab your package.

She and I hadn't ever spoken, but I loved to listen to her speak with others. She was an older German woman with a thick accent. She knew everything that went on in town, and loved to share what she knew. It hit me that since our first interaction with the local congregation of God's Own, I hadn't spoken to a single person who wasn't either a member of my family or a member of the congregation.

Still high from my new feeling of free will, and probably just as much from my first coffee, I looked over in her direction and said," Hello."

I wasn't joking earlier when I said it's hard for me to make eye contact, I was looking in her direction, but sort of to the left of her head and slightly past her.

We had a conversation. It was my first conversation. My first real, non-God's Own or family conversation, was with an older German woman who ran the post office. We talked about the weather. I mentioned how great the field smelled. I told her I was just getting over a cold and everything smelled new to me. She laughed. She had a deep belly laugh. I really wanted to be able to laugh like that. I left the post office but didn't head directly home. I walked across the street so I could walk along the field. That side of the road didn't have a sidewalk, just a ditch. It wasn't wet, so I just jumped down to the bottom of the ditch, mail in one hand, coffee in the other, and started to walk back in the direction of the trailer park.

I looked for a break in the corn, a way in and through. I found a few, but it was the middle of the afternoon in bright sun, and cars kept driving by. I didn't want to try any of the ways in and have someone see me. I just made a mental note of where they were, for later.

By the time I was across the road from the trailer park I had finished my coffee. I ran across the street and tossed the empty cup in a dumpster they kept behind a billboard sign. That sign never made sense to me, it was an advertisement for the trailer park. The trailer park was very visible from the road. The trailer park manager had an office that was maybe ten feet off the road.

Why did they need a big billboard to advertise it? Maybe it was just a place to hide the dumpster.

It took me another few minutes to walk back to the trailer. As I walked up the porch and reached for the door, my new confidence waned. My hand was inches from the doorknob and memories flooded in. Not just of Friday, but of my entire life in that trailer. Years of abuse. Years of torment. Years of frazzled nerves, tension, and overall defeat. It was hard to keep any sense of free will and confidence in the face of those memories. The doorknob was a siphon, stealing that free will and replacing it with every horror I'd experienced. I limply gripped the knob, opened the door and walked inside, looking at my feet. Grady was on the couch, playing a video game. Jeremiah was sitting on the floor watching the game being played on the TV. I walked across the room and dropped the mail on the kitchen table, then walked back across the way I'd come and headed into my bedroom. I shut the door. I grabbed a book, and I started to read.

Before I knew I could escape to other places, books were my escape. I'd read their pages, and in my mind, I was there, in them. It was like I wasn't seeing the words on the pages. I wasn't even just seeing the events in my mind. It was more like I was in the story. It wasn't a special ability. It was just a very used and practiced imagination. My one escape. Books were my shield, my defense against my life. They were my only true friends. Epic fantasies were my favorite. Anything that was at least a thousand pages long, full of dragons, dwarves, elves, and giants. Dwarves were always my favorite race from fantasy books. Of all the races they were the ones I wanted to be friends with. They weren't about pretense or judging. They loved to work hard, and when their work was done, they would party just as hard. Their families were tight knit. They protected each other, they would fight for each other, they loved spending their time together. I was drawn to them because they represented the family, the normalcy, I ached for.

I emerged from the book when Mom got home. Her coming through the front door jolted me from the story.

Through the door I could hear her ask, "Is he back yet?"

Grady responded, "No. We haven't seen him all day."

"Well, if he isn't back here by the time I get home from work tomorrow, I'm calling the police."

I heard her go back to her room and shut the door.

Fourteen

It was Thursday before she called the police. I don't believe the delay was intentional. I think she was losing her grasp on time. Her depression had gotten so bad that she was ignoring all three of us. She'd go to work, she'd come home, she'd go to bed. She wasn't even getting up for dinner any more. We were on our own. With her lackadaisical about everything, and with Hal gone, the trailer had an eerie, empty, feel to it.

I'd continued to get the mail each day that week, after my coffee from the convenience store. I made a point to converse with the clerk at the store – his name was Finley but he said to call him Fin – as well as the woman at the post office. When I wasn't doing that, I was in my room, reading. Grady and Jeremiah had their routine down, too. They would pass the controller between each other and play video games all day. We made our own food. Mom must have been eating at work, because she wasn't eating with us. We had lots of sandwiches and macaroni and cheese.

When the police did arrive Thursday evening, I stayed in my room. I stopped reading. I wanted to listen, but I didn't want to meet them. I didn't want to answer questions. I wasn't a liar. I didn't know how to lie. If they had asked me if I knew anything, or asked me when I'd last seen him, I wouldn't know how to handle it.

They were there about thirty minutes. Mom and Grady told them about the open window and the screen pushed outside.

Grady told them Hal had been sneaking out and hanging out in the abandoned school. Mom told them Hal failed his freshman year, and about all the fights he had in school, the truancy issues. I heard the police mention teenage runaways. They said they'd check out the school. They said they'd stay in touch and asked Mom to contact them if she heard from him.

Was it really that easy? Hal was gone. He was dead. I was responsible, and instead of an investigation, they were calling him a runaway? It was perfect.

Fifteen

The next few weeks I took it easy. Pain and blood told me I was pushing my healing body too hard. In the morning I'd get up and get a shower, get some cereal, and be back in bed before Grady and Jeremiah were up. Once Jeremiah was awake and out of the room, I'd turned on my small book light and read. I kept the blinds in the bedroom lowered all day, even though Mom didn't monitor compliance with the rules any more. I didn't get up for lunch. I started to get the mail every other day, so I didn't have to walk those few miles so often. More than the walk, I missed the coffee. I knew I was going to have to get more money; a dollar a month doesn't cover a thirty-five-cents-a-day habit for long. The twenty-five dollars I started with wasn't going to carry me forever.

I wanted more than anything to get out to that field at night. Practice my abilities, see what I could do, test my limits, that sort of thing. I had high hopes and was eager to start. However, I knew that until I was fully healed, snaking my way through a cornfield would be dangerous. If I slipped or fell, I could tear open my wounds again. Then who knew how long I'd be delayed?

In those few weeks I hardly saw Mom at all, and I don't remember talking to Grady or Jeremiah. Mom would be gone for work before I'd get up for my shower. When she'd get home after work, I'd be in my room reading and she'd go straight to her room to sleep. She didn't even acknowledge Grady and Jeremiah when she got home. Their entire life consisted of sitting in front of the TV playing video games. I never heard them go outside, but they always seemed to have new games. I wondered if they were finding a way to sneak out, though it was odd that if they were, because it would mean they hadn't realized sneaking wasn't really needed any more. Unless it was me they were trying to keep in the dark from their activities. I had suspected that Hal had broken into other trailers for alcohol and any money he could find. It was possible those two had been breaking in and stealing video games.

I was reading the same stack of books over and over. Mom hadn't taken me to the library in some time. All I had at that point were some books the librarian had let me keep because I'd checked them out so many times and no one else had borrowed them in years. I had never actually spoken to the librarian, but she seemed like a kind person. I think she could see something in my eyes. She never tried to force me to talk like some other adults. I think she understood some more of our situation than others did. Maybe she had some knowledge of God's Own. I was more thankful than I can find words for when she gave me those books; other than religious books I'd never owned any before. Owning that small stack meant that I had permanent access to escape to other worlds, worlds where I could live with my dwarves. I knew that once school started again, I'd be able to get books from the school library, and I'd have new places to visit.

Mom just slept. Saturday mornings I'd do some cleaning around the trailer, but I'd grown very lax about it, and it showed. My brothers did nothing to help. It was summer vacation, and their routine didn't differentiate by day of the week. On Saturdays I'd have a shower, eat breakfast, do some light cleaning, then read. I was never hungry, so I ate little. I had grown nervous again and it affected my appetite.

It wasn't the same kind of nerves I'd had before. Before, it was fear of pain, fear of anger, fear of family, fear of the world, fear of God's Own. It had become fear *for* my mom, not *of* my mom. Even after everything she'd done and said to me, I remembered my love for her. It wasn't something that faded away like what I must have felt for my brothers at one time. I missed her, the her from California, the her from before the playground.

I'd read enough books on the subject and gained enough knowledge in school to believe she was mentally ill, which meant that the things she had done weren't entirely her fault. What she did was wrong, but I didn't think she understood that. In her mind, the world worked in a certain way. At some point there was a snap in her way of thinking, and she tied all bad things in the world to me. It was like she had this map of worldwide events and used string to trace back every negative action to me. Of course, that doesn't make sense, but when you're mentally ill I guess things make a different kind of sense than they do to everyone else.

I blamed God's Own. If it was obvious to a fourteen-year-old what was going on, surely they must have known too. Instead of getting her help, or at least trying to talk to her about it, they stoked her beliefs. Not about me in particular. To my knowledge then, she hadn't shared her thoughts about me with them. They stoked her fire and brimstone perception of everything. She was the *Armageddon is coming's* poster child.

I was surprised that none of God's Own came to check on us when we stopped attending the meetings. Prior to Mom's depression causing her to sleep all the time, we had attended every meeting for years. Often my brothers no longer went, but Mom and I were always there.

The sleeping all the time, the depression, it was like a flare shot in the air to signal mental health issues. When I had that realization, it made me think back on the events of my life. How she used to be a loving, caring mom, then the hollowness that would occasionally seep in, followed by the fiery anger. Then those times grew more frequent and would last longer. Then it was like she'd been replaced and all that was left was the fire. Then the fire burned out and there was a walking zombie who could only sleep when not at work.

It was all mental illness, not just the depression. I was positive that if anyone had just identified what was going on early enough, everything in my life could have been avoided and she could have been helped. Our whole family could have been helped. Instead, no one did anything. Instead, when it got to the point that it should have been obvious to everyone, they all just seemed to think she was a religious zealot and didn't want to intervene in any way for fear of her retribution.

It started small, but the more I dwelled on it all, the more I grew to hate everyone. Everyone she'd been around in the years this was going on. How was it that not one of them sought to help her? They knew she had four children at home. They must have known our environment was bad. No one did anything.

I don't mean to say I hated everyone in the world. I just mean I hated everyone who sat on the sidelines because they were too cowardly to face her and make her get help. Mental illness isn't something that gets better on its own, it spirals and spirals and only gets worse. She needed treatment.

I ran so many scenarios in my mind of how I was going to try and talk to her about it. A few times I even built up the courage to do it. I went to her bedroom after she'd get home from work. I'd tap on the door, slowly open it, and say a few words. Either she'd be out cold and snoring, or she'd just be lying on her back with wide open eyes staring at the ceiling. Most of the time she hadn't even changed out of her work clothes. She would just lay there on top of her blankets fully clothed. When she was staring at the ceiling, I never saw her blink. I don't think she was conscious of me being there. She never responded. After a series of attempts I gave up. I had little hope that I'd be the person she'd ever listen to.

I hated God's Own. I had never shared their beliefs. Internally, I questioned and disagreed with everything they taught. I always followed their teachings because it was what I needed to do to survive. As bad as my life was, Mom would have been so much worse if I had outright refused to follow God's Own. Along with God's Own, I hated Mom's family. I didn't know any of them, didn't know their names, didn't know what they looked like, but I hated them to my core. Why did they disown a single mom with four children? Did they know about her issues? Was it easier to cut her out than to face the problem head on? Didn't they know that in disowning her, they were condemning four children to that horrible life? Whatever rift had happened between them, there was no excuse they could give that would let me forgive them for abandoning us.

I was a constant rush of emotions. Between changing hormones (which I'd learned about in health class), identifying my mom as being mentally ill, realizing some of my special abilities, the mental and physical abuse, that final weekend with Hal, watching my brother die at my direction, and the constant battle between newfound confidence and ongoing nerves and fear, I was a wreck. If either of my remaining brothers had bothered talking to me, they would likely have thought I was a maniac. Maybe I was.

Another fear I was realizing was that mental illness can be

hereditary. There was a good chance that was what had happened with Hal. I didn't care. What he'd done to me, it didn't matter whether he was mentally ill or not. I couldn't have him around after that. Really, if he could do that to his own brother, what was he going to do to strangers when he had the opportunity? For that matter, what *had* he done to others? I knew from overhearing conversations between Mom and the principle at Hal's school that he had been fighting all the time. Violence was his path. A path I cut short.

I tried to undercut the war of hormones and emotions with logic, but it didn't really help. Logically, I knew that even though Hal had done horrible things to me, I should feel some sort of remorse or regret over what I'd done. I didn't. In fact, anytime I thought about it, anytime I'd visualize that night in my mind, I smiled. I couldn't help it. And I thought about it a lot. It was like reading my favorite book in my mind over and over.

Sixteen

Once I felt I was fully healed, I started getting the mail daily again. That was sometime in July. So much had happened, and so much more was going to happen.

Me and my routines: I'd get up, shower, eat, go back to bed, read after Jeremiah left the room, get the mail early to mid-afternoon, come home, go back to my room, and read. Around that time, I'd stopped eating dinner. Breakfast was my one meal.

When I'd get the mail, I'd take my time with the walk. I'd admire the abandoned school for a while, meander past the few houses that were on the street. I'd get to the convenience store, occasionally taking a table after pouring my coffee so I could have a longer conversation with Fin. He was a dark-haired man with even darker eyes. He was one of those guys whose age was hard to guess. He could be anywhere from mid-thirties to late forties. He loved to talk about movies. I didn't know anything about movies, but I loved hearing him talk about them. The way he would talk to me, as if I were just some normal kid in a normal life, I didn't think he understood that the kindness I felt from him was often the most positive piece of my life. As the days went on, I wanted to spend more and more time sitting there, drinking coffee, listening to Fin.

Some days I'd walk along the railroad tracks for a while instead of heading straight to the post office. The tracks were lined by thick trees on both sides. It gave me an eerie but exhilarating feeling to walk on them, looking straight ahead. The tracks were so straight, they looked like a never-ending line framed by never-ending trees. Once I made my way to the post office, I'd make conversation with the clerk as much as I could. Sometimes she was just too busy, stuffing mail into the boxes or telling some other customer about a new piece of gossip she'd come across.

She was that person who would start many sentences with, "Now, you know I'm not one to tolerate gossip about people, but..." Then she'd air everyone's dirty laundry. I often wondered what she told people about me.

On my way back home, I always walked along the cornfield, in the ditch. I'd started to carry a little notebook and pencil I found in a drawer in the kitchen. I made a little map of the edge of the cornfield. Using the few houses across the street as landmarks, I marked on my map where I thought the openings were that I should check out. I wasn't sure if that much effort was really needed, but I also wasn't sure how much light there would be at night. I wanted to try and give myself every advantage I could.

I chose a Monday night for my first excursion. I figured there would be less chance to be seen sneaking around the field then. If it was the weekend, people would have been up later, driving down the road from the bars. I figured they'd all turn in at a reasonable time on a Monday for work on Tuesday. I stayed in bed pretending to sleep until midnight. I had learned a bit from Hal, and left a bag tucked outside with clothes and shoes. Instead of sneaking through a window, I just used the backdoor. I was worried at first, since it was just across from the bathroom, which was right next to Mom's room. I opted to go for it though. She didn't wake up when I was in her room trying to talk to her, so I guessed she wouldn't wake up if she heard a quiet noise from outside her room. At most, she'd probably think it was one of us using the bathroom. Another benefit of the backdoor was that it was out of site from Grady. The windows in the living room and kitchen were all in his sightline. If he had been sneaking out, there would be a chance he'd be awake too. If he saw me, I was hoping he'd just think I was in the bathroom.

    I'd tested out the door a few times the previous week, so I knew that I needed to grab the handle tightly and lift the door as much as I could before opening it, otherwise it would stick. The door opened outward and there were small plastic steps just below the door. I stepped out, lifted the door again, and closed it. I didn't want to leave it unlocked in case someone happened to wander by, so I grabbed Mom's keys before I left.

    My clothes bag was stashed by the shed, under some wood. The back of the shed was blocked from the view of the other trailers near ours, so I changed clothes there, stashed my pajamas in the bag, and hid it back under the wood. Instead of walking out the front of the trailer park, which was well-lit, I went under the electrified fence and through the cow pasture. I could have avoided it, but I chose to make my way to the abandoned school. It was a reminder of what I could do, a reminder that I had a reason to be confident. I didn't lallygag. I made my way back under the fence near the road. The spot I came under the fence was strategic. There were no streetlights and no houses. If no cars came by, there would be no light for anyone to see me. I felt like a spy. I crouched down, low to the ground, and bolted across the street. Remember that I was new to free will and excited. That's probably why I decided to commando roll into the ditch once I was across the street. I thought it was the cool thing to do. Looking back, I'm surprised I didn't get impaled by some random stick.

I did bring my little cornfield map with me, but it was too dark to see it. I hadn't brought any type of light with me. I was too scared someone might see it and call the police. It didn't matter that I couldn't see it since I'd memorized it. I made my way to the first entry option and squirreled in, still hunched. At about four feet in, I realized that the opening didn't really have any type of path behind it. Just many, many stalks of corn. I made my way back out and continued to sneak in the ditch down to option two. Same thing. Just like it was the same thing with the third, fourth, and fifth options. I'm guessing anyone who knows anything about farming would know that just because a few stalks of corn are missing at the edge of a field, it doesn't mean it leads to some sneaky path. It probably just means something knocked down a few stalks at the edge.

I decided to stop looking for a path. I was so small that I figured I could just wedge myself through until I could find an opening. Again, looking back, it was a stupid thing to do. Any number of horrible accidents could have happened to me that night. Or I could have become disoriented and lost and stuck out there. I was stupid about stuff like that. As it had been a few times, luck was on my side. After twenty minutes or so of squirming through what felt like an endless supply of stalks, I was in an open area. I know nothing about farming, so I have no idea why that open area was there. Maybe there was a soil issue, maybe it was something about irrigation, I haven't any real idea. It was a little sunken below the rest of the ground, by about three feet. It sort of looked like a half-acre crater in the middle of the field. It was grassed over and relatively flat inside. I thought it would be a good place to start. It didn't look like anyone would be able to see me, or anything else, in the crater with the corn guarding any view.

I was wearing a dark-gray hoodie, which I took off and wadded into a ball. I lay down in the middle of the crater and rested my head on the balled-up hoodie. I closed my eyes and I pushed out. It was so easy, didn't take any effort. I just had to decide to do it, and then do it. As I was each time before, I was in the cracked earth place. The cat creature with the alligator mouth and too-big-for-its-body paws sat there, tail flipping behind it. It was looking at me. I mentioned before that it was about twice the size of a large bear. Sitting, its head and shoulders raised up and it towered over me.

I was still unsure exactly what the Dark Woman was or how she was getting in my room. I hadn't called her from one of these other places, I hadn't seen her in one of these places, she would just appear in my room. I had a feeling she was from one of these places, particularly due to her similarity with the Glowing Woman. I wasn't sure if I was calling her in some way that I didn't yet realize, or if she was something else entirely.

What I did know was that I had successfully called this cat in the past, as well as the Glowing Woman. When I'd done that, they had not appeared directly with me when I was back at my body. Instead, they just showed up when they were needed. I wanted to practice bringing one of them with me, to be at my side immediately. Not because I needed them to do anything, like guard my house or kill my brother. Just to be with me. It would be my first of many tests.

Even though I didn't know anything about who or what it was, I felt a fondness for, and closeness with the cat. The loneliness in me was enough to stagger anyone, but when I was near that cat, I felt a kinship strong enough to strangle that loneliness. It was the first of these beings I'd drawn out, the first to protect me. I didn't mind its stare—it didn't feel threatening.

Slowly I walked up to it, getting a better sense for its size. It kept its eyes on me. As I crept closer, I was able to hear it purring. I reached up a hand to touch it. I stopped when its mouth started to open, just slightly, and close, quickly, over and over. It made a chittering sound. I thought maybe it didn't want to be touched, so I lowered my hand. The purring and staring resumed.

I started to talk, not knowing if it could understand me or not.

"My name is Hezekiah, but I go by Hez. I don't know exactly who you are, but I never thanked you for what you did in California. Thank you, for protecting my family. I don't know exactly who was on the roof, or what would have happened to us if you weren't there but thank you.

I'm trying to figure out what I can do. I'd really like you to come with me. I don't need you to do anything. I just want you to come to this field I'm in. It's safe. No one else is there, no one would be able to see us."

The cat didn't move.

"I'm going to go now. I really hope you'll be there when I sit up. If you're not, I'll be back though. I'm not, like, threatening you or anything. I just mean I'll be back to try again. Thanks again, if you can understand me and everything."

I was back at the crater in the field. I lifted my head then propped myself up on my knees. I looked around the crater but didn't see anything. There was little moonlight available to see by, but I was sure I was alone. I lowered my head, disappointed in myself. I couldn't believe I thought I could make it work. Then I heard the purring.

I looked up, directly in front of me. I could hear it, but I couldn't see anything. I squinted, trying to see better in the dark. It was there! Right in front of me, but I could barely see it, even as it walked right to me. The night was dark, as was the cat's fur. It was like it was blending in the shadows. No wonder the neighbor in California didn't know what they were seeing. I'm surprised they were able to see it at all.

My eyes nearly teared. I was struck with a blow of happiness. It was wonderful. It was real. I wanted to do something, and it worked. I wanted to hug that cat, but instead we just sat there, looking at each other, for several hours. I hadn't slept, but I wasn't tired. I was so wired from the feeling; my confidence had become a tornado inside me. I was proud of myself. It was a foreign sensation.

I knew that I needed to give myself time to get back through the field, across the street, through the pasture, to the trailer, change clothes, and get back inside before Mom got up for work. Otherwise, I'd have to wait until she was gone, and that would increase the odds that Grady would hear me coming back inside. I did weigh that as an option. I figured even if he did hear me, he probably wouldn't confront me or say anything. We'd gone the summer so far without talking, why start then? But I didn't want to chance it. It was all still too new.

No sooner did I think about traveling the distance to the shed, than the cat lowered its head and pressed its forehead to mine. The shadows quickly smudged all around us, and suddenly I was behind the shed, the cat next to it.

Just as suddenly, without giving any thought to what had just happened, I said in a hushed and hurried voice, "Thank you! You can go back now!"

Then it was gone. My immediate thought wasn't that this creature had seemed to just teleport us all the way home, but was that it would be seen, seeing as how it was practically as tall as our shed. Once it was gone, that's when it hit me. The cat, it melds with shadows and teleports. The Glowing Woman, she killed with a scream, and then she evaporated the whole mess it caused with light that came from her hand. Did they have other powers? Did all of them have powers?

I had more questions than answers. That night proved that I could bring them over, even when I wasn't in some direct need. Also, that I could bring them over without a delay. That was enough for the first test.

Seventeen

For the rest of the summer, I went out three nights a week for my tests. Usually one of those nights I just spent with the cat. Sometimes in its cracked earth place, sometimes in the field. I tested the teleporting ability. I discovered that the cat could teleport just me to places while it remained elsewhere, and I could then release it to go back to its place just by thinking it instead of saying it out loud. Most of the time, the cat came with me wherever it teleported me to. I preferred it that way.

I wanted to test the distance of a single teleport, so I thought about Antarctica. Again, I was stupid. I didn't even have a jacket on, just tennis shoes, black track pants, a t-shirt, and my hoodie. First off, when we appeared in Antarctica, we were about twenty feet from a research station, where probably five people were looking directly at us. I can't imagine the stories they tell about some scrawny red-headed kid in dark clothes showing up with a giant black cat out of nowhere. Second, we were standing there for two seconds when I felt like I was going to die. The cold was a stabbing knife, and it was so sudden and shocking I thought I'd pass out immediately. My breath was lost as soon as we appeared. I don't remember even being able to think of anything, much less the field, but either I did, or the cat just knew I needed to get out of there, so it touched its forehead to mine and we were back in the field. It took me a good thirty minutes to warm up again.

Another one of my tests was to try and figure out how many of the other places there were. Every time, I started in the cracked earth place. I could walk around, but if I looked and focused a bit, instead of walking, I would zip to a new place. When that happened, it looked like everything around moved past incredibly fast. Then suddenly it would all stop, and I'd be in a different place.

There was a night where all I did was travel to place after place in rapid fire succession. I visited over a hundred places that night. In some I could see the dweller of the place immediately. In others I didn't see any.

One of the first I went to that night was just dark open space. I wasn't even on any type of ground; I was just floating. I imagine I looked a lot like what the Glowing Woman looked like. In front of me was a green glowing ball of light. It was very round, and its diameter was about that of a love seat. Its intense green light made my skin look green. Floating there, being a different color, I felt like an alien.

Another was a treeless swamp. The ground was mushy and covered in a foot or more of water. There was vegetation growing in and on the water. At some point in my life I'd developed a fear of things underwater, so when I saw a very large wake headed in my direction, I zipped to another place.

That was when I met The Healer. I didn't know if any of the beings I was seeing had names or not, so I'd started giving them my own: Dark Woman, Glowing Woman, The Healer, Big Green, and so on. I didn't want to call the cat The Cat, so I gave her a real name. I never looked for gender, but at that point I just had a feeling she was a she. I wanted her to have a strong, nonhuman name, like the characters in the books I read. I decided on Vrail-Thuune. Most of the time I just called her Vrail.

Anyway, The Healer. He was in a cave at the top of a mountain, sitting cross-legged. He was one of the largest beings

I'd seen so far. The cave was huge, and he filled much of it. He was the size of a two-story house. Instead of green or brown, like a frog, he was gold. I don't mean he was made of gold; he was just that color. I had no fear when I looked at him. He didn't look at me. His eyes were shut and his hands rested on his knees. He looked like he was meditating. That day I wasn't calling any of the beings to the field – I just wanted to keep zipping from place to place to get an idea of how many there were – so it wasn't for another week or so that I pulled him out and discovered he was a healer.

From the cave I just went from place to place for hours. There didn't seem to be an end. I never ended up in the same place twice. For the last fifteen minutes or so, I did test my ability to go to a specific place. That was another successful test. I thought about Big Green and then I was back floating in the dark space. I thought about the Glowing Woman and I was back in the dead forest. Then I had an idea. I thought about the Dark Woman.

I was back in the field, but not in my body. I was looking at my body, resting on the ground. The Dark Woman was standing above my body, her dress tucked behind her, her toes practically touching the top of my head. Her head was turned down, just staring into my body's face. It was a terrifying sight. I thought about Vrail and was back in the cracked earth place. She wasn't sitting. She was pacing back and forth, hair hackled on her back, mouth chittering, tail flipping. She saw me and pounced. Not on me, but in one leap she was next to me. She was looking me over from head to toe, head bobbing all around. Much of what I knew, I didn't understand, but I knew absolutely that she was worried. I started wondering if the bond I felt wasn't just one-sided, but maybe she felt it too. Had she felt my spike of fear when I saw the Dark Woman over my physical body?

I knew I needed to go back to the field, but I was terrified of what would happen. Would I open my eyes and see the Dark Woman above me? Had she done something to my body in the field? Could she do anything to my body? Vrail poked me in the chest with her alligator snout. She was starting to calm down even though I wasn't.

I went back to my body in the field. I was trembling and immediately clutched shut my eyes. I noticed I was holding my breath. I forced myself to breathe, but my throat kept hitching at the effort. I shot my eyes open and threw my stick arms in front of my face. They would be a meager defense, but it was a gut reaction to what I expected to see. Instead, I didn't see anything other than the open, dark sky. I sat up and looked all around. No Dark Woman in sight.

I hustled back to my stash of clothes, changed, and got back inside the trailer. When I was back in bed, I thought over what I'd learned that night. There were more of the other places than I could reasonably remember, and no signs of an end to them. Even though I didn't see a being in every one of the places, it seemed logical that they all had a being in them. Vrail had started to show signs of emotion toward me, which was entirely new. Then the Dark Woman. I tried to see her place and instead I was sent to see her standing over my body. I couldn't figure her out. She was a puzzle piece that seemed to belong to a different puzzle.

Eighteen

It was near the end of the summer when something horrible happened, and it was my fault. Most of my tests had been successful and I learned a lot. Mostly about specific places I could go and the beings within those places. I had also learned that if I brought a being back with me, all I had to do was ask them to show me what they could do, and they would. For the most part, I didn't have any fear about doing that. It had all gone so well that I thought of them all as friends, or guardians. I figured that most of them had multiple powers, like I'd seen in Vrail and the Glowing Woman, but when I asked to see their powers, they would show me the more benign things they could do, not the dangerous things. I'd even gone back to the swampy place and sight unseen brought its being to the field. It was a giant snake, the kind of giant snake that people talk about seeing in the Amazon.

When I asked what it could do, it coughed, and a fist-sized, spherical, glass ball shot out of its mouth. I picked up the ball and held it in my hand. It started to glow with a clear, bright light. I meant to toss it up and down in my hand, like a baseball, but when I tossed it up, it didn't come back down. It just hung in the air, and lit the entire crater. It was such a weird power, but I loved it.

I don't think I'd grown cocky. It was more that I'd grown comfortable and confident. My home life hadn't changed. Mom was still sleeping all the time when she wasn't at work, and I had no relationship at all with my two brothers, which was fine with me. Going to the field and zipping to the other places was all I really had. It had become the escape that my books used to be. I felt a closeness to these beings, I trusted them. Then the thing with Big Green happened.

I hadn't brought Big Green out yet because it was so bright. I didn't want to take a chance and have the owners of the field see it in the distance and come out to investigate what was going on. Then I had what I thought was a near perfect alignment of factors. I'd heard from the post office clerk that the farmers who owned the field were going on vacation to visit their son in Florida, we were due to have a bright moonlit night with no cloud cover, and there were going to be several local bonfire parties as a last hurrah before summer ended and school started again.

At first everything happened as I'd expected. I got to the field, pushed out, hung out with Vrail for a few minutes, moved on to the dark space place with Big Green, and came back to the field with it. It was hovering incredibly low to the ground, and it was indeed bright outside, so I felt we were safe. If anyone had noticed the light, I figured they'd think it was one of the bonfires. But then I asked it to show me what it could do.

It hummed. I'd never heard anything that sounded exactly like it did, but the closest I can come up with for the sake of a description is a theremin. I had heard one in a school music class years before. I was amused. I thought its ability was some sort of music. Then the farmer's house exploded in the distance. It was a large, three-story farmhouse. I didn't actually see the house explode, but I did see the giant fireball from that direction. Then, there were explosions all around me. All around the field, on the road, from the direction of the trailer park—they were everywhere, some small and some large. Then, one right next to the crater. That's when I saw they were rocks coming from the sky. I don't know enough about rocks to say whether they were asteroids, or meteorites, or just boulders conjured to the sky, but they were big, and I thought they were destroying everything.

As soon as I got my senses back, I yelled," Go back! Go back! Go back!"

Then Big Green was gone.

As soon as Big Green was gone, the rocks disappeared, but the damage they'd caused did not. I had to get home, and quickly. I dropped to the ground and pushed to Vrail's place, and quickly brought her to the field. I thought of my bedroom and was teleported there directly, then I mentally released Vrail to go back to the cracked earth place. I was standing there, still in the dark clothes I wore to the field, the window bright with the numerous fires outside, and Jeremiah staring right at me.

Nineteen

The day after that incident, I walked to the post office, dwelling on what had happened the previous night. What Big Green did was distressing enough, but knowing that my brother saw me appear in the room made it worse. He hadn't said anything afterward, just glared at me for a few seconds before he heard all the screaming outside. He and Grady both jumped up and ran outside, neither saying a word. Mom didn't stir. Or, if she did, she didn't come out of her room.

I quickly changed into a set of pajamas, stashed the clothes I had been wearing under the bed, and then headed out myself. There were sirens and people screaming in the distance. It looked like there might have been flames coming from the other end of the trailer park, but we couldn't see anything other than a flickering radiance above the row of trailers in the middle of the park. I heard Grady and Jeremiah whispering but I couldn't make out what they were saying. After a few minutes they walked back into the trailer, not sparing me a glance.

I stayed out for another few minutes, half wondering if there was something I should do to help, and half expecting the police to storm our trailer looking for me. It made me think how disappointed they would be, the officers who had helped us when they found us homeless in a car on the side of the road. They would be disappointed at what I had done, accident or not.

When I went back inside, my brothers were already back in their beds, though I doubted they were asleep. Jeremiah said nothing as I got in my bed. He didn't say anything to me the rest of the night, or the next morning. Maybe he thought he was dreaming. Maybe he didn't actually see me appear out of thin air, maybe he thought he happened to look over just as I was getting out of bed or getting back in after a trip to the bathroom. Before heading out to get the mail, I made sure to linger a little bit in the living room, watching them play their video games. I wanted to give an opportunity for it to come up. Nothing.

I stopped at the convenience store before the post office. As normal, Fin was behind the counter. I wouldn't have said we were friends, but he and the post office clerk were the two people I spoke with the most. Maybe I did think we were friends, but I doubted he did. He was an adult and probably thought I was a weird kid who didn't have friends.

I said," Hey." I walked in and headed right to the coffee pots. I had decided to have a seat to chat a bit—I had no intention of rushing to get back home. I wanted to find out what kind of damage had been done, what kind of damage I had done.

As soon as I set the paper cup down on the table, Fin knew I'd be staying to talk, and started in immediately.

"Did you hear what happened? It's so freaky! Did you see any of it?"

"I didn't really see anything."

Lying felt a little easier than I had expected, but I felt bad lying to Fin.

"My brothers and I heard yelling outside after whatever happened, so we went outside. It looked like there might have been some fires, but mostly we just heard sirens and people yelling. Does anyone know what happened?"

"It's so weird, so many people are saying the same thing. I don't get how the sound of the impacts didn't wake people up."

Fin was looking outside. Maybe he was lost in thought, maybe he was looking at a small crater on the other side of the street.

"Impacts? You mean something hit us?"

My stomach was in knots. I hate lying.

"Dude, you didn't hear? They were rocks, but they don't know where they came from or where they went! Like, they don't think they were from space or anything, they said it was more like debris launched from a volcano, but we don't have any volcanoes here. Also, the fires they caused burned themselves out really quickly. Even weirder, all the rocks just disappeared! The damage was localized to the impact sites, hardly any damage to the surrounding areas or buildings."

"Was there a lot of damage? It didn't look like much other than some small burn spots between the trailer park and here."

That was the first true thing I'd said to Fin that day.

"No, that's another weird thing. The only major damage was that farmhouse in the field across the street. It's a good thing they were gone, down in Florida visiting their kid. Guess they'll have to find somewhere else to stay when they get back. I did hear they might just stay in Florida a little longer now."

I wasn't in any way thinking about heading back into the field anytime soon, but it was good to know that if I needed to, I could without worrying as much about being seen.

"I just, I don't know, I mean, what do they even do? How do they even figure out what happened? Were people hurt? You said there wasn't much damage other than that house, but what about people?"

I had wanted to push the fact that I didn't know what happened, and I really did wonder how anyone would try to figure it out, but until it came out of my mouth, I hadn't even thought about the possibility of someone being hurt.

"Not that I've heard about, but I guess you never know. They didn't do like a town sweep knocking on doors or anything, but I don't think anyone's been reported hurt or missing. Maybe if someone is, the police just aren't saying."

I grabbed my cup, went to the counter, paid, and told Fin I'd see him later. I headed outside and started walking to the post office. When I got there, Miss Zelda, the post office clerk, was in a tizzy chittering with half a dozen other people all pressed up to her cage. I still have no idea if Zelda was her first or last name, but when I felt confident enough, I had asked her what her name was. She gave me a hard side-eye through the bars of her cage and told me to call her Miss Zelda.

I didn't ask any questions since so many others already were, but I hung out at the back counter listening for information. It seemed like none of them, even Miss Zelda, had any more information than Fin. No large amount of damage other than the farmhouse, no lasting fires, no one knew the cause, but they were guessing it might have been a local weather phenomenon. One of the colleges from St. Louis would be sending some of their researchers out to survey the area and start a hypothesis for study.

I left the post office and instead of heading directly home, I decided to walk out to the park on the edge of town. It only took about two minutes since the town really consisted of one main street and one cross street. There were a few small dirt roads, but those were for farm access, not really what anyone considered town. The park was just a big open space with two baseball diamonds, one small basketball court that doubled as a tennis court, and a large, unmarked field that could be used for football. No one else was around when I walked up to the only set of bleachers and took a seat. I don't remember even thinking anything at the time. My mind was still numb and trying to process what had happened. I just stared out at one of the baseball diamonds. I remember a blank mind, then being hit with a thought. I had that second ability. I could see things in the future if I tried. I could just look forward and see what was going to happen. I had been so taken with visiting the other places that I didn't think about seeing the future much.

I set my coffee down on the bleachers, dropped my hands to my side, closed my eyes, and pushed. I pushed forward, not out. It's hard to explain. It's like, pushing out moves me, pushing forward moves everything around me. Pushing myself out takes me to a different place, pushing forward takes me to a different time. Out could take me to the dry cracked land with Vrail, forward would let me see what was coming.

When I'd intentionally done it before, I was focused on Hal. It hardly took any concentration. I knew who I wanted to see, and I knew what I wanted to see, and I saw it. This wasn't the same. I focused on the town, but I didn't see anything other than the town as I had always known it. There was nothing special. No answers, no new knowledge or insight. I came back and opened my eyes. As normal, I was confused. I hadn't really practiced with that ability the way I had with my other one. I thought that maybe I was trying too broadly. Maybe it worked with Hal because I was focused on one person. Similarly, back to the earliest time I could remember, it was about that girl on the playground, not the whole school.

I closed my eyes and pushed forward again, but that time I focused on Fin. I knew that if anyone would get the full scoop in the future, it would be him or Miss Zelda, and really, I just liked Fin more. Maybe because he was the first person to see me and treat me like a person. Most people looked right past me, or worse, saw me with pity but didn't think I was worth the effort to help.

I saw Fin. I saw the future, but it wasn't what I expected. Whatever was happening was in the congregation of God's Own. The view I had was from the stage. The seats were all full. I couldn't see any faces. They were all in robes and cloaks with hoods pulled over their heads. I looked to the left. Fin was on his knees on the floor. Not on the stage, but just before the steps leading to the stage. His hands were behind his back, maybe tied there. He looked up. Half his face was covered in blood. Tears running down his cheeks left little rivers running through the dried blood. Mouth taped shut.

I came back, opened my eyes, and threw up on the bleachers. I'd forgotten to eat my cereal that morning, so it was all coffee. Bitter, acidic, frothy, and disgusting. Coming up, it looked exactly how it had going down, but it didn't taste anything like it. I took a split second to consider pulling Vrail to get me back to the convenience store as quickly as possible, but after what had happened with Big Green, I didn't want to risk pulling any of them, so I jumped up and ran. It took less than a minute to get there. I body checked the door, causing it to fly open. Fin had been turned the other way, stocking cigarettes, when I bashed through the door.

He jumped, screamed, "Fuck!" loudly, and spun around, eyes huge. When he saw me, his expression changed from surprised anger to concern and he asked me what was wrong. He walked around the counter and headed toward me. When he was a few steps away, I saw him look up over my shoulder. His jaw dropped. Before I could turn, I saw the same spots I saw when Hal choked me unconscious, then everything went black.

Twenty

I was disoriented when I woke. At first, I thought it was just another normal morning and I was waking up in my bed, but with an axe buried in my head. I had never had such a bad headache before. I opened my eyes but my surroundings were blurry. I couldn't seem to focus. I started to remember what had happened. I had been at the convenience store. I was there because of the future I saw about Fin, then I saw spots, then I woke up in the congregation.

I was in the basement, zip tied to an extremely uncomfortable metal folding chair, facing a cinderblock wall. I could hear shuffling behind me. The light was dim and I couldn't turn my head enough to see who was causing the noise. There was little light coming through the small windows set high in the walls just above ground level. The light looked faintly red, like early evening.

Fin, I started to think about Fin. I tried thrashing around to get the chair to move so I could look for him. Being naturally physically weak, on top of whatever they had done to me, the little metal chair didn't move. I heard more noise behind me, but still couldn't see anything. I wondered if they had Fin back there, and if they did, what were they doing to him. My mind raced. Why had they taken me, or us? Did they want Fin? Did they want me? Did they know what I could do? Is that why they drugged me? Did they want both of us? The questions in my head wouldn't stop.

I tried to push out. I was going to get help and get us out of there. It didn't work. Every time I tried to push out, the feeling of an axe in my head got worse. The more I tried to concentrate on pushing out, the harder it got to concentrate. It got so bad I almost passed out again. My eyes swelled, but I didn't cry.

"Good, it works."

I heard the voice and knew it was the overseer.

I tried to talk, to ask what had happened, why I was there, but my throat was so dry I just chortled an unintelligible rasp.

"Give him some water."

My eyes were still having a difficult time focusing, but I saw a yellowish blob appear at my side. An arm stretched out, holding a clear glass of water with a straw sticking out of it. I wrapped my lips around it and drained the glass dry.

I cleared my throat a few times, then screamed.

"Where is Fin? What did you do with Fin?"

My voice cracked over and over, I couldn't control it.

"Don't worry, Hez. Your father is fine."

Immediately, all I had running through my mind was *What the fuck did he say?*

"You know I don't know my father. I'm not asking about him, I'm asking about Fin!"

I was sure the overseer was messing with me, trying to keep me confused.

"I know everything you don't know, and I know everything you do know. Don't worry, I'm not going to keep you in suspense. I'm going to give you a condensed version to get you up to speed. Then we have a request for you. That's why you're here. If you help us, we can talk later and I can give you all the tiny details I'm sure you'll be after."

He was so calm. He sounded no different than when he was

giving a Sunday morning talk from the congregation podium.

I stayed silent. I couldn't concentrate, and I had no idea what to say, or whether I should even believe what he was getting ready to tell me. I knew all the members of the congregation. They all willingly lied to push their beliefs onto others to get what they wanted.

"This all started in 1976 when your mother met Fin. She'd already had two boys with another man, an abusive man whom she left, but Fin didn't care. He wasn't from a particularly well-to-do family, but he had a landscaping job that provided a steady income. In early '77, your mom became pregnant with you. Immediately, we received signs about you, of your importance. You probably haven't realized it yet, but you're not the only one with gifts. Our group receives signs about some of the gifted. It lets us track and monitor those who might be helpful to our cause. When needed, we get them to further God's work here on earth. They are his gift to us, to God's Own.

We knew you would be powerful. We knew you could be a key part of the end of things. We didn't know exactly what you'd be able to do. One of our members has abilities that you would call telepathy. She can use her ability to read minds or to control them. After your birth, we periodically sent her through your mother for information. Initially she would just read her mind. Occasionally we needed to take control. I won't go into the details of why, but we needed to divide your parents. Our telepath made your mother do something Fin would never forgive. She made your mom cheat on Fin with her abusive ex. She became pregnant with your younger brother.

She left Fin but he wanted to fight for custody of you. We made your mom flee with you and your siblings to California, then we used our influence here to shut down his case for custody.

We ruined him, left him jobless, homeless, friendless, made sure no court would believe he could support you if he were ever able to find you. We even provided witnesses stating they saw him abusing your mother and older brothers, which we leveraged into an order of protection, prohibiting him from any contact with your family. In California, we kept your mother from getting a job. We paid your family's meager living expenses. We needed to make sure she was available to have eyes on you at all times. Mostly we just had our telepath monitor your life through your mother. We didn't expect your powers to start manifesting so early, so when they did, we took control of your mother and tried to scare you out of developing or using them.

We're still unsure why, but your mother's mind became more and more difficult to control. She was lapsing into states that prevented us from controlling or reading her. Eventually, we took control completely to make sure we didn't lose our footing. When you were getting old enough, and we thought you'd be able to exert some control over your abilities, we brought you back here. We needed to see what you could do.

Since your family arrived, we placed our people everywhere in your life. Of course, this congregation is ours. We also placed our people in your trailer park, in your school, all over town. We know what happened with your brother. We know what you've been doing in the field. We've been recording it all. It quickly became clear why we need you, what we need you to do."

Finally, he stopped talking.

"Are you done? So, first off, I've never believed one word from your talks, and I don't believe one word of anything you just said. If you have a telepath, then why control my mom and not me? If I was so important to you, why would you put me through all of the abuse I've been through. Why would you isolate me instead of taking me in? Why would I ever believe some random convenience store worker is my father? He could be anywhere in the world, and you think I'm going to believe that my father just happens to be the guy who works down the road from where I live, and that I talk with him nearly every day, and that he's never thought to mention, 'Oh, hey, maybe you don't know this, but I'm your dad.'"

I tried to sound sarcastic, but I just sounded childish and scared.

"Belief in what I tell you is irrelevant. What matters is what we need from you. If you choose to help us, we will change your life for the better. If you don't, we will kill Fin while you watch, then we will find a way to take control of you and make you do what we want."

That was the first thing he said that I really believed.

"And just what is it you want from me?"

"Do exactly what you've been doing out in that field, and bring us a specific being from one of the other realms."

He spoke like nothing could be simpler. Like a neighbor asking to borrow a cup of sugar.

"What being is that?" I didn't really need to ask; I knew he was attempting to be dramatic. I knew he was predictable. I knew what he wanted before he ever said it.

"God."

He said it in that haughty and self-righteous way that meant he believed there was no way I could ever have guessed that he, the overseer for God's Own, would ever mean God.

"You predictable fuck."

Twenty-One

After he laid out the full master plan like any generic paperback villain would, he left the basement. I heard others leave with him and was left in silence. I assumed it meant I was alone. I sat there and thought about everything he'd just said. I didn't even consider any of it being true, at least not the stuff about Fin. I tried to figure out why he'd throw that lie at me. He wanted some reaction from me, but I couldn't figure out how that would get him the reaction he wanted. The other stuff I believed, probably a bit too quickly. The stuff about controlling my mom and the stuff about wanting me to raise *God*, or whatever it is they claimed was God. It made sense. If I had special abilities, why wouldn't others?

I heard the rusted basement door slowly screech open but I was facing away from it so I couldn't see anything. There were around a dozen steps leading from the door to the basement floor. I heard a hard, loud, thump come down each of them. My mind flashed to some of the books I'd read, books that were more solidly in the horror genre than fantasy. I imagined some pale giant slowly walking down the stairs, dragging a huge hammer behind him. I imagined a cloaked woman wrapped in chains attached to heavy, spiked, metal balls. On the last few steps, I heard a quiet grunt follow each thump. After the final thump, something was dragged toward me. It was slow, it was careful, it grated on the floor like nails on cement. I figured that they didn't get whatever reaction they wanted, so they were going to club me in the head and be done with me.

My vision was still a little blurry, but improving. From the corner of my eye, I did see a cloaked person, but I couldn't tell if they were a man or woman. The hood effectively obscured their features while the robes and cloak obscured their body. With one hand trailing behind them, they dragged a chair. In it was Fin, bound arms behind him, mouth taped shut, dried blood that had run from his scalp down half his face. Take away the chair and add the tear stains running through the blood, and he would have looked exactly as he had when I pushed to the future. If I hadn't run to the store, if I was alone when they took me, would he still have been safe? Was I the reason he was there?

Once he was placed directly in front of me, the cloaked chair dragger left and shut the basement door.

It's hard to explain the emotions that hit me so abruptly. Most of my life, I'd been beat down. The world and everyone in it were very much against me. I had been destroyed mentally and physically. I was always alone. Then, as I realized what I could do, and I realized I could defend myself – maybe *avenge* myself is the better phrase – I gained some confidence. Not a lot compared to other, normal people, who hadn't been through what I had, but enough that I wasn't constantly a scared little boy any more. I'd started making choices for myself. I knew that if anything got too rough, or too scary, I could pull one of the beings from the other places to help me. Now, this person I was sure I considered a friend then, was in front of me, bound and bloody, looking right into my eyes, and there was nothing I could do. I was just the scared little boy again, waiting for the next crushing blow.

I mentioned before that I didn't have tears left. That still held true. My throat grated and my eyes burned, but I didn't cry.

"Fin, I'm so sorry, everything is my fault. I'm why you're here and I'm why you're hurt, and I can't do anything. I'm sorry, I'm so sorry Fin."

My throat was like sandpaper, every word scraping more pain.

He couldn't talk with his mouth taped shut, but he continued to look in my eyes. He tried to speak, but I couldn't make out any of his words, then I saw his tears begin. My heart hurt. It was so sudden. My emotions often seemed so dull after everything I'd been through, but as soon as I saw those tears, I physically ached. I asked him if he was in pain. He shook his head no, still not releasing my eyes from the darkness of his. That's when I realized why they brought him.

"Are... Fin, are you... are you really my dad?"

I paused and started. How do you ask a person you hardly know if they're your father who never bothered to tell you they were your father?

Initially I didn't see him move. After a few seconds I saw his head bob so slightly up and down I thought I was imagining it.

Even with his mouth tightly held shut, I heard the words, "I'm sorry."

Logically I know that at this point someone came back to the basement and took us both up to the main hall of the congregation. They dropped Fin at the foot of the stage and they brought me up on the stage, next to the podium. I can't give any details, because I don't remember any of it. I remember that slight nod from Fin, then I remember being on the stage, tied to a straight wooden stake mounted in some sort of concrete, or heavy, base. My hands tied above me, my feet below me.

I was looking down at Fin, exactly as I was when I pushed forward. I looked to my side and then looked up. Someone was there, hammering a nail through my hands and into the stake while another did the same with my feet. I was being nailed to a stake on a stage while dozens and dozens of members of the congregation just watched. I was in shock. Kidnapped, drugged, no access to my abilities, at everyone's mercy again, Fin.

Fin. Why hadn't he told me?

I couldn't feel anything. I just looked around, over and over, like a bobblehead toy on a dashboard. Fin screamed through the tape. Not words, just pain. He hurt because I hurt. I could see him scream, could see the pain we shared, but I couldn't hear him. It was all so slow. Everything felt dampened. All I could hear was hammer on nail. That was the soundtrack for the horrible show. How was it, all of it, my life, why did everything have to be so bad, so hard, so painful all the time?

Twenty-Two

Slowly sound came back, things started to pick up to normal speed, and the pain from the nails in my extremities hit. Before I could scream out, the members of the congregation near the back jumped up and ran forward, yelling as they flooded toward the front. As they ran, some of their hoods dropped. Those who had been in the very back row still sat there, but were missing their heads. Some of their limbs detached and fell to the ground. Most of their bodies stayed in place, but slumped against each other.

Several of those running toward the stage started to run slower, like they were suddenly trying to wade through something thick. They changed color, taking on dusty, dirty hues. Then they burst. They burst into sand that just dropped, loose, to the floor, every bit of them. All that was left was their clothes. Everyone was screaming. More heads flew off bodies, random limbs and chunks of torso seemed to slice off and drop to the ground. No one was near them. Heads flying, people turning to sand. Everyone's screams drowned mine. I didn't know what was happening, but suddenly there were only a handful of the congregation still in one piece, and they all crowded around me on the stage. Fin was still on his knees.

The glass doors between the side entry and the main congregation opened. Two young women walked in, twins. They were dressed in identical light-gray outfits with black trimmings. They had the darkest skin I'd ever seen. They were beautiful. If angels exist, they surely look the same. They stood in the back, behind the farthest row, the row with the bodies missing their heads.

The overseer was at the corner of the stage, surrounded by members of the congregation. One of the men, whose hood was down, had their hand planted solidly on the overseer's shoulder. The man looked at Fin, and only Fin, amidst all the chaos. Next to me, one of the others dropped their hood. It was Miss Zelda. Some sort of clear knife appeared in her hand and she held it to my throat. Another one, a tall spindly man, dropped his hood and held a similar weapon to Fin's chest.

I was weak, I was in pain, I was confused, I was scared, but I was starting to concentrate again.

The overseer spoke first.

"Thread, Dust, I wasn't aware you'd be joining us tonight. If I'd known, we might have prepared differently."

I wasn't looking at him, but I could hear the forced smile on his face.

"Well, we do like surprises." The twin on the left spoke. Her voice was deep and rasped, it was hypnotic.

"We'll kill him now. We've waited this long. We can wait for another."

His voice never changed. He still sounded like he was giving a Sunday talk.

The twins looked at each other, crossed their arms, and gave each other a small, side-mouthed smirk. Then they looked back at the overseer.

"What? You don't believe me? I'm hurt, after all we've been through together."

He nodded at the one who was threatening Fin. The man leaned down so his face was inches from Fin's face. He lifted up one arm and placed it around Fin's back. Under other circumstances it would have looked like the start of a loving embrace. Then I watched him slowly bury the knife in Fin's chest. I screamed. My blood was on fire. Miss Zelda flinched but didn't lower her weapon from my throat. The twins just stood there; smirks still clear on their faces. The embrace lasted around thirty seconds before it was released and Fin slumped to the ground, his dark eyes open, but empty.

Suddenly, the man who took the life of the person who might have been my father, started to shake. He shook so quickly that he became blurry. The blur came back into focus, but it was no longer the man who had stabbed Fin. It was Fin in that man's clothes. I was baffled. Was Fin some sort of shape shifter who had pretended to be a member of the congregation? If so, who was the man who looked like Fin who he had just stabbed? What… the… hell?

I was done. I was done with all of it.

The same twin who spoke earlier spoke again.

"Want us to finish this?"

Now it was Fin's turn. He said, "No Thread, I think Hez has this now."

He had been watching me since he unblurred, his dark, dark eyes examining mine. He saw that for a few seconds my body was there, but I was not in it.

Quickly, the overseer turned his head and screamed at Miss Zelda, "Do it! Do it you idiot! Do it now!"

It was too late. Vrail tore through her like rice paper. Before Zelda's arm, head, and torso hit the ground, Vrail was pouncing on the group surrounding the overseer. The person who had their hand on the overseer's shoulder touched the wall with their other hand and a large black hole appeared. They both flew through it and it closed as suddenly as it opened. But before they flew through,

I could swear the man looked at Fin and mouthed," I'm sorry." It was all less than a few seconds and they were gone. The remaining members of the congregation were in pieces around me.

The twins ran toward the stage. Fin, still not unlocking his gaze, took a step up toward me. Quicker than I could keep up with, Vrail was in front of me, elongated snout snapping at all three of them. Then she let out a roar that made the building shake. All three of them stopped in their tracks. The twin's smirks were gone.

None of us moved for what felt like minutes, but I'm sure was just a few seconds. I knew what I needed to do. I knew Vrail would understand. She sidestepped next to me and placed her mouth in front of me, still keeping an eye on the other three. She dipped her head down, and with her teeth grasped the nail holding my feet in place and gently pulled it out. Then, she raised and did the same with the nail in my hands. I dropped, very weak, onto her shoulders and back. Immediately, the two of us were in a thickly wooded area near a small clearing. I don't know why, but Redwood National Park in California was the only place I could think of.

Twenty-Three

The first thing I did was pull The Healer while Vrail stayed with my body. I pulled him to the clearing—there was nowhere within the trees for him to fit. Once I was back, and the frog was cross-legged in his normal meditating pose in the clearing, Vrail helped me onto her back and softly carried me over. I slid off and lay on the ground, just a few feet in front of the golden frog. Vrail backed away into the woods, but kept her eyes trained on me. I didn't sense any fear from her, but her concern strongly emanated its way to me. Once she was entirely into the trees, she disappeared, but I knew she was still there, invisible in the shadows.

    I lay there and The Healer sat there for several minutes. I didn't feel in danger of dying anytime soon from the wounds I'd been given, but I was in pain. It was difficult to tell whether the physical or mental pain was worse. Being sucked back into the helplessness, not being able to defend myself, cut at me, but not as deeply as the story about Fin. If it were true, I could be happy to have a family connection outside of the family that made every attempt to alienate and hurt me. But was that really their fault if God's Own was controlling Mom? Or I could be angry, livid, furious, that he had left me in that situation. He clearly had some sort of power. He must have been able to help me, and just chose not to.

    The trees around me began to wither. It was like the transition from summer to fall to winter, all in a dozen seconds or so. As they withered, the frog began to glow brighter, illuminating the clearing that had been darkened under the night sky. He opened his eyes and looked down at me. A soft light focused out of them and onto my body. He had taken life from the trees around us and was directing that life into me. I began to heal. Wounds closed, bruises lightened and then disappeared. My body was fixed, but my mind was still reeling and felt cracked and splintered, each splinter thinking in a different direction, each direction with its own expanding questions splintering further.

I was physically OK, but still covered in drying blood. The frog raised his giant hand above me and I began to float, until I was standing in the air directly in front of his head, high above the ground. He slightly split his lips and blew on me. The blood, the grime, the sweat, it all seemed to fly off me as he blew. At the same time, my clothes began to come clean and be refreshed too. It was like I'd just stepped out of a warm shower and put on clothes fresh from the dryer.

He lowered me to the ground, but not on my feet. His hold on my body felt like thousands of flies walking all over every bit of my skin. It gave him control over my limbs and joints. It wasn't something I could fight against. I didn't even try. When I was back on the ground, he placed me in the same meditative, cross-legged position he sat in. Then the feeling of the flies all over me was gone. He had released me.

I placed a palm on the ground to lift myself up and walk away. Quickly his hand was above me, the flies returned, and I was pushed back into the meditative position. We repeated this twice more. In frustration I almost released him, but I also wondered why he was being so insistent on keeping me there. His hand lowered and rested on his leg, as his other hand was on his other leg. His eyes had closed immediately after I was healed, his breathing was deep and slow. I thought that maybe he wanted me to meditate. It wasn't something I'd ever done before, but I figured I'd give it a try and see if he'd let me go afterward.

I closed my eyes and tried to take my breaths in line with his, deep and slow, holding that full breath in for several seconds before allowing it to slowly slip back out. For the first few minutes my mind didn't slow. I was still frustrated, angry, and had too many questions in my mind to stop thinking about them. Then, I realized that the more I focused on my breathing, focused on keeping it in sync with his, the less space my mind had to think about the other things. I held that state, just focusing on my breath, and after some time even the thoughts of my breath were gone. My mind was blank, my deep, slow breathing had become automatic. I don't know how much time passed, I wasn't aware of time, or anything, in that state.

When I opened my eyes, the frog was gone and it was high noon. I could tell by the placement of the sun. I felt like I'd slept for a week. I couldn't remember feeling so physically or mentally refreshed. I quickly realized that the frustration, anger, and innumerable questions were still in my head, but it all felt manageable. I was calm. Serene. I was in a beautiful surrounding. The trees which had been used to heal me had come back to life.

Vrail was curled up at my side. My clear mind let me start to devise plans to deal with the events of the previous day and the information that had been presented to me during those events. I knew that I would need time to decide exactly what to do. I felt no urgency to act on anything immediately. For several hours I just sat there with Vrail, watching nature around us.

Twenty-Four

I had Vrail take me to a nearby town. Once there, I found a small store and bought a few spiral bound notepads and a pack of pencils. After that, I had Vrail bring me back to the clearing.

I needed to write everything down, I needed to keep track of it all, hoping things might get clearer, hoping it might help to answer some of the questions and help form a plan of what to do next.

That's what this is. I've written down everything that's happened to this point, as I sit here on a tree stump on the edge of this clearing. Vrail is still here. I don't fear anyone finding us. If anyone does, she can just disappear into the shadows. Her presence helps me stay calm and grounded. She reminds me that this is all true and not just in my head. Writing it all out, it sounds like a fantasy, a dream, a nightmare, unreal in every way. But this is my life and I've tried to list everything pertinent so far. Before setting my pencil down I'm going to list the questions most prominent in my head. Tomorrow I'll start working on how I can get answers.

1. Is Fin my father?
2. What was that power I saw Fin use?
3. If he's my father, why didn't he ever help me?
4. How much of what my mom put me through was God's Own controlling her?
5. Is my mom still there at all?

6. Can I help my mom?
7. Have my brothers been controlled in the same way?
8. Who or what is the Dark Woman?
9. Does anyone know I am missing?
10. Does anyone care that I am missing?
11. How many people have special abilities?
12. Where do these abilities come from?
13. Which being does God's Own think is God?
14. Where did the overseer go?
15. Is all of God's Own in on this, or just the one congregation?
16. Why did they nail me to a stake?
17. Who are Thread and Dust?
18. How are they connected to Fin?
19. Where am I going to live?
20. Where will I get food, water, and shelter?
21. Where will I get money?
22. Do I really want answers, or do I just want to disappear?
23. Am I crazy?
24. Why me?

PART TWO

One

I haven't written in a month. I wanted to plan for what to do next, how to get answers, how to figure everything out. I will. I'm not giving up on that. I had more immediate needs that need tending. Though they weren't on the top of my list – food, water, shelter, money – it became clear quickly that those needed to be my priorities.

Vrail is still with me. I wouldn't have survived this past month without her. Our connection has gotten stronger.

The first few days were rough. Though The Healer helped me physically and mentally, a clear mind didn't make me knowledgeable about the kind of survival skills that would allow me to live in a forest. I couldn't find water, couldn't find food, couldn't start a fire, couldn't build shelter. I knew that I could pull some of the beings from the other places to do some of those things, but I was still hesitant after what happened with Big Green. The last thing I needed was to start a massive forest fire. Then I would really be responsible for one of those things Mom always blamed me for.

By the second day, it hit me that Vrail might be able to help with those things. I trusted her. I trusted only her. I was so thirsty, it drowned out the hunger. Instead of asking her to take me to a specific place, I asked her to take me somewhere away from humans, but where I could get drinking water. She took me to a stream. I don't know if the stream was still in Redwood, or somewhere else in the world entirely. But when I needed to get more water, that's where she would take me.

That first time at the stream I just dipped my hand in to bring water up to my mouth. We stayed a while, at least long enough for me to quench my dry throat and get hydrated again. I realized that I'd need to get containers to hold water so we wouldn't have to go to the stream every time I needed a drink. Then I wondered where I'd keep containers. It put me back on the idea of shelter.

Again, I didn't ask Vrail to take me anywhere particular. I just described what I wanted. I asked her to take me to an abandoned but safe cabin, somewhere that had no humans around. She took me to the cabin we've been staying in. It's bigger than I expected. When I think about cabins, I think about small, one room, log type places where the wind blows right in and everything is covered by leaves and dirt. This place is nicer than that, but clearly abandoned. It has a large open space downstairs. When you walk in, the kitchen and dining area is to the right. To the left is a large open space with a huge brick fireplace in the back wall. The front wall and the wall around the fireplace are all built in book shelves. They were all empty when we got here, though. The upstairs has a bedroom, fully walled in with a large, thick wooden door. The other half of the upstairs is an open loft with a desk. I guess it was meant to be an office area. There are large windows in the bedroom and the loft, but they're small compared to the windows in the open area downstairs. The front of the home is solid wood, but the side walls of the cabin are nearly entirely windows.

Vrail comes inside with me. She can't comfortably fit upstairs, but she loves to curl up in front of the fire downstairs.

After that, it was just working through immediate needs. I'm not proud of a lot of this, but I'm doing what I need to survive. I couldn't hunt for food, and even if I asked Vrail to do that, I wouldn't know how to prepare anything. I couldn't forage, I wasn't prepared for that either. One wrong berry or mushroom and I could be poisoned. Sure, I could chance it and hope that I could pull The Healer if something went wrong, but what if I wasn't fast enough? Or what if I died in my sleep?

I waited until night and had Vrail take me to a grocery store. I made it clear that the store needed to be closed and empty of all humans. I had found some clothes in the cabin, not much, but what I needed. A black t-shirt I was able to fashion over my face with a few rips in it for my eyes. In case they had security cameras, I didn't want my face on film. I knew that Vrail would be hidden in the shadows, so her coming with me wasn't a concern.

The cabin doesn't have water, electricity, or gas. It's shelter and nothing else. I grabbed some pots and pans, a few of those long fireplace lighters, and as much food as I could carry that wouldn't need to be refrigerated. Cereal, powdered milk, spaghetti noodles and jars of sauce, apples, oranges, stuff like that. I grabbed soap, shampoo, and some other toiletries. Near the pots and pans section, I found a small appliances aisle. I really wanted a coffee pot, but I knew it wouldn't work without electricity. I found this thing called a French Press. You just put the ground coffee in it, then pour in hot water, and then you press this filter down from the top. It said it was better than a drip pot, so I got it and five bags of already-ground coffee.

Once I was loaded up, Vrail took us back to the cabin and I unloaded everything into the cabinets of the kitchen. I ate dry cereal and a few apples while I lit the fire for the first time. It was the first time Vrail curled up in front of it. I don't know if she slept. As close as we are, I don't know if she needs to sleep. Or eat, or drink. I've never actually seen her do any of those things.

Next, I needed clothes, newspapers, and money.

I decided that instead of having Vrail take me places to steal stuff, I would have her take me someplace I could steal money. I know it isn't a moral thing to do, but I feel less horrible stealing from a bank that's fully insured and is sure to get its money back, than stealing from some store that might depend on every single sale to keep its staff employed and stay open.

It was really smooth, I put my t-shirt mask on, gave Vrail the parameters of a closed bank that had money in a walk-in safe we could both fit in, make sure no people were around, that normal stuff. The place she took me to was huge, like, we were just in this huge walk-in safe, and it was bigger than any house I'd seen in person. The walls were lined with all these boxes, and there were tables that just had stacks and stacks of money on them. I started wondering what kind of bank it was, because it wasn't what I expected. I really hadn't expected it to work at all. I didn't know if banks actually had walk-in safes or if that was just something created for fiction.

Anyway, I had a sack with me and I grabbed random fistfuls of money to fill it. I was ready to go, but before taking us away, Vrail hit all the stacks of money with her tail. They had been tightly packed with rubber bands in these neat, large, stacks. She hit all of it as I watched, a little shocked. Money flew everywhere, just rained down. If the money had been placed in any type of order on the tables, that order was out the window.

When we got back to the cabin, I counted the money. I'd grabbed more hundreds than I'd expected. I didn't really pay attention when I filled the sack, I just grabbed from random stacks. All in all, I'd ended up with just over $300,000.00. It didn't look like a lot in front of me, but it totaled so much more than I thought I'd ever see. I was almost sick.

The next few days Vrail took me all over the country. I asked her to avoid any state that was in any way physically connected to whatever state the bank had been in. I bought new clothes, cast iron pots and pans (the cheap stuff I took from that first grocery store burned up in the fireplace), and every newspaper and magazine I could find.

For weeks we've followed a routine. I wake up in the

morning and go out to a small lake we found near the cabin and I have a very cold bath. Instead of the lake, I still use that first stream for drinking water because I read somewhere once that you should not drink from stagnant bodies of water. When I get back to the cabin, I heat up water in the fireplace, then add some cold water to the powdered milk and add that to some cereal. About the time I finish with my cereal, the water in the fireplace is hot enough to add to the coffee in the French Press. After I finish off the coffee, Vrail takes me many places to buy more and more newspapers and magazines. I spend my days reading them, looking for any reference to me, Fin, God's Own, anything that might shed some light on my situation. So far, I haven't found anything.

One day I was so frustrated that I just couldn't read another paper. I had Vrail take me to a bookstore. When she takes me places during the day, she sends me on my own. She always sends me behind a building, or into a public restroom, someplace like that where I won't be seen. Then, when I'm ready to go back to the cabin, I find a place she can come get me without being seen. Then she appears and takes me back to the cabin. She can teleport me somewhere without coming with me, but she can't teleport me back from any distance.

Once I was at the bookstore, I bought one of everything in the fantasy section, one of everything in the horror section, and one of everything in the classics section. I didn't go to the sections I just went to the check out counter and explained what I wanted. The woman behind the counter just laughed at me. I pulled out a stack of money and her laugh stopped. She asked how I'd be getting all those books home. I told her I'd pay extra if she could box them up, and just before closing put them in the alley behind her shop. It took some convincing – by convincing I mean an additional $200.00 – for her to agree. I told her that my parents were shopping in the town and had asked me to find books to stock the library in our new house. I don't know if she believed me. I don't really care. I hung out in that small town, I think it was called Red Wing, all day. There were several little coffee shops I decided to try out. There were so many antique stores I couldn't have made my way through all of them if I'd spent a whole weekend there.

When the shop closed and the sun had gone down, I called Vrail to meet me in the alley. Once she took us back to the cabin, with the boxes and boxes of books, I started to unpack them and order them on the empty shelves. It took hours, but that was just because I kept stopping to read the descriptions on the back of many of them. I kept out a small stack of about a half dozen that I wanted to start sooner rather than later.

I did something similar with a furniture place. The cabin had a tiny bed in it that I'd been using, but it was soft as rocks and killing my back. I bought a new queen-sized bed and frame, some nightstands, a couch, a few chairs, some end tables, a kitchen table and chairs. Standard stuff to make things a bit more comfortable.

I was able to set up everything downstairs just fine but being so weak made setting up the bed upstairs a bit difficult. It just took more time than I wanted it to take.

At one of my stops, I bought a handful of oil lamps and a bunch of candles. It was getting cozy.

That gets me to last night. I was sitting in the living room, reading a book, when I asked myself what I was doing there. Sure, I needed some stuff to survive, but did I want to give up on ever getting answers and just live there with Vrail? Or did I want to find Fin, find answers?

Most of what I've done for the last month has been procrastination. Putting off the inevitable. My immediate needs were taken care of in those first few days. Now I'm just avoiding what I need to do, because it isn't going to be easy.

Last night, I put real thought into why I had avoided coming up with my next moves. I kept coming back to Fin. As much as I wanted to know more about my abilities, more about God's Own, more about Thread and Dust, I mostly wanted to know more about Fin.

I am terrified to find out whether he really is my dad. If he is, then he abandoned me. He left me to suffer for nearly fifteen years. If he's not my dad, then I'm alone. Back to having a family who hates me.

I can't risk having Vrail take me directly to him, so I've decided I'm going to try and use my ability in a different way. The last few times I used it to see the future, it seemed to show me things that I was going to witness in person. When I saw what the Glowing Woman was going to do to Hal, it was from my vantage point in that hall of that old school. When I saw Fin, it was from my vantage point on the stage. I thought back to the girl on the playground—even that was from my vantage next to the school. That's why if felt like déjà vu in the beginning. I really was seeing the same thing twice.

Tonight, I'm going to try something different. I'm going to concentrate on Fin, but in the present. I don't know if it will work, but if it does it'll be a way of collecting information without putting myself in immediate danger.

Two

It worked. Now I have more to think about.

I'm coming to understand my ability better. I think it's one ability that lets me do different things. It's all based on moving my mind, or whatever you would call my non-physical being. I can move it to other realms, times, and locations, maybe even into other people.

Last night, when I was ready, I took the meditation pose The Healer had put me in. I followed the pattern of deep breathing he taught me. Once my mind was clear, I focused on Fin. Not on him as I would see him in the future, but just him in the present. I wasn't trying to put my mind in his body or anything—that felt dangerous without practice. Instead, I was trying to place my mind close to him.

I've become used to instant gratification with what I can do. Going to the other realms, seeing the future, it was natural and easy. This wasn't. The first few attempts I made just didn't take. My mind did go somewhere, but it wasn't anything I could recognize, or even really describe. It was just a lot of shifting colors in different shapes. They seemed aggressive. Like, if everything was made of rainbows, rainbows that shifted colors constantly, and if all of them were fighting each other. I know that doesn't capture exactly what I saw, but I can't do any better than that.

The fourth time I tried was different. At first, I couldn't see anything. I had cleared my mind, and then I started hearing whispers. They weren't really whispering, more like muffled talking. As if someone was in a room with a closed door and I were listening from outside. The sound got clearer, and as it did my eyes focused until I had sight and sound.

I was in a room faintly lit by a few lamps with soft glowing bulbs. I looked down and I could see myself. I was in the black suit, with the nice watch and fox-head tie pin that I have on whenever I go to one of the other realms. There was a small bed in a corner of the room. A desk, stacks of books and papers were everywhere. Set against a wall was a chest that had been chained shut. There was a small clothes dresser, above it was a mirror. Standing in front of it, looking into the mirror, was Fin.

He turned and looked right at me.

"Hez." His eyes watered as he said my name.

I took a step away. Could he see me?

"I'm sure you're confused, but please don't go, we have so much to talk about."

He took a step toward me and I rushed away. I backed into the bed and fell back onto it. I could feel it. It wasn't like just my mind was there, it was like my actual body was there, but I knew it wasn't.

Fin stopped moving toward me, but still had a hand stretched out toward me.

"What's going on, how can you see me? How can I feel things? I'm not really here!"

I think I'll always be the poster child for confusion.

"It's all right, no one else here will be able to see you, just me and your mom. To see you, someone must be directly, physically, related to you."

"What… what did you say? Mom? Did you say my mom is here?"

I was going to lose it.

"She is. After what happened at the congregation, I sent Thread and Dust, along with another person I trust, to get her and your brothers. I knew God's Own would try to get her as a bargaining chip against you, and given your strained relationship with them they would probably try to recruit your brothers against you. So, yes, your mom is here. But something is wrong. All she does is sleep. We've been feeding her through a tube to keep her stable. We're trying to figure out what is going on. She's going to be OK, she's safe here. We will figure this out."

His eyes still watered. His eyes are so dark, they just radiated sorrow.

"My brothers, can they see me when I'm like this? They're directly related to me."

Of course this wasn't a question from the list I wrote, but I felt it important enough to ask.

"Maybe? Probably? I guess I don't know. They would be directly related to you as half-brothers, but I'm not their dad, so I'm not sure."

He did seem genuinely unsure.

I was still sitting on the bed. The shock of him seeing me was wearing off, and I was there to get information. I needed to ask questions I wanted answers for, instead of just reacting to the situation.

"Tell me, honestly, in one word, are you my father?"

My voice was steady. I didn't want him to hear it crack.

He didn't hesitate. He answered, "Yes".

"Why did you leave me? Why didn't you come get me?"

"What the overseer told you is true, but there's more to it. When your mother and I met, I didn't know anything about this part of our world. This part where some people have special abilities. I'd never heard of God's Own. I didn't know any of it. When I met your mom, she was the kindest person. I hadn't known much kindness before her, to me it made her a beacon. We fell in love. She became pregnant with you. Then it all changed. At the time, I didn't understand any of it. Just a week before I found out she was pregnant, I found out she cheated on me. Just once, but it was with my brother, Patrick. I nearly ended things, but then found out she was pregnant with you and that I was your father. We reconciled and in the following months moved in together.

You were only a few months old when I came home from work one day. She was sitting in a chair in the kitchen. She had a blank look on her face and flatly told me that she'd cheated again, had sex with her ex, she was pregnant with his child, and that she was leaving me and taking you and your two older brothers. I ran to your room, but you were gone. I ran to the room your brothers shared and they were gone. When I got back downstairs your mother was gone. That morning, I'd gone into your room to check on you before leaving for work. It was the last time I saw you in person until you walked into the convenience store in Lankon.

I went everywhere I could imagine she might have taken you. I called the police. I called a lawyer. I called her family. I called all her friends. No one knew anything. The police were the worst. They wouldn't do anything. Said that she was your mom, we weren't married, so it wasn't kidnapping."

At that point, his eyes weren't just watering. Tears ran down his cheeks. He didn't sob, he kept his voice in control, but I knew it was painful to remember this story.

I wanted to walk over and hug him, to comfort him. I didn't. I continued to sit on the bed. He continued to talk.

"I tried everything I could, for years. Every time I thought I was making progress I would suddenly get blocked. It was just one thing after another. I was laid off, I ran out of money, I lost my home, my lawyer wouldn't represent me anymore, I couldn't afford the private investigator I had trying to track you down, the police entirely ignored me. For a stretch of time, I was homeless.

I made my way to St. Louis. Slowly built up a life again. I worked for a newspaper, just maintenance stuff. It was all I could do to support myself. I had no idea where your mother had taken you, so I had no idea how to find you. I had no idea what you were going through. What you would end up going through."

What he told me made sense with the story the overseer gave me. Of course he was blocked at every step. God's Own had blocked him.

"What's your ability? What was that you did in the congregation?"

I had so many new questions, but I made myself stay on the questions I had already plotted out.

"My ability is passive, not active like yours. That just means that it isn't something that I can control, or just make happen. The short of it is if someone kills me, I come back, but in their body. Their body is reformed to look like me. Doesn't matter whether it's a man or woman, or how old they are. I reform to look like me at the age I am at the time."

His tears had stopped. I think it was easier to talk about abilities than about me.

"And what happens to the person whose body you take?"

"I don't know. We have found lots of records on the abilities that some of us have. That's how I know your mom and I can see you now but others here can't. But this ability of mine, it isn't mentioned in anything we've found yet. Most of the abilities mentioned are the powerful ones. A lot of the minor abilities aren't mentioned. It could be that there is some active piece to what I can do, but that I just haven't figured it out yet. Your ability has been confusing us too. Your mind shifting has been documented by some in the past. It's rare, very rare, but not unheard of. However, no one has ever been able to bring back the beings from the other realms. There are many who believe our abilities come from those beings. Like, each of us is tied to one of them. When we are tied to one, we get access to their special abilities. You being able to bring them back, being able to have them use their powers, gives you every single power that every single one of them have. It's entirely unheard of."

His voice was getting excited.

"So, I'm the freakiest of the freaks?"

I chuckled while I said it. I wasn't asking it for an answer.

"You're the most wonderful of us."

He sounded proud. I think. It wasn't a tone I'd heard before when anyone described me.

There was a knock on his door, and it startled us both. He jumped at the noise, and I jumped back to my body. I opened my eyes to see Vrail curled on the floor. She opened one eye to look at me, closed it, and purred.

Three

I took a few days to consider everything. Between the rant from the overseer and the explanation from Fin, I'd had a lot of exposition to consider. Do I still call him Fin? I think so. I think I believe him, but maybe it's just that I want to believe him. I have so many more questions for him. For others too. Right now, I'm worried about my mom. I still have so much anger and hurt for what she put me through, but if it's true that it wasn't her and it was some person from God's Own controlling her, I should help her. I don't know how though. Maybe I can take The Healer to her? Or can I ask Vrail to bring Mom to me, then pull The Healer?

    I still only had the word of the overseer and Fin to go on, so before I continued any further, I wanted to investigate a few things, to confirm or disprove what I could. I changed clothes, filled a tumbler with coffee, and had Vrail take me to the old, abandoned school in Lankon. I had Vrail come with me but wait in the shadows in the school while I made my way to my family's trailer. Since I was going to a populated area, I did this at night.

    I came out of the part of the field right next to the shed on our lot. As I came around the corner, I noticed the back door was slightly open. Not swinging wide open, just slightly open in the frame. I looked back to the school, wondering if I should bring Vrail with me into the trailer. I decided not to after all, for all I really knew my mom and brothers could be in there, asleep. Wouldn't that be a terror for them, waking up and seeing a giant black cat with an alligator snout chittering at them? Not to mention, I did not think she'd be able to fit inside.

I made my way to the door, sipping my coffee, and carefully opened it. Once inside, I lifted the door slightly and closed it all the way, locking it behind me. The trailer was quiet. There were no lights on inside. I walked the few feet to the door leading into my mom's bedroom and slowly pushed it open. Even in the darkness I could tell she wasn't there. I flipped the light switch, but the room stayed dark. There was no power. I made my way to the bed and lay down, pushing out. I was in the cracked earth place, but Vrail wasn't there, obviously, because she was still in the school. From there I went to the treeless swamp and pulled the snake. I haven't named the snake yet, but I really should.

Once I was back in my mom's room I stood up. The snake was coiled and filled half the bedroom. I'd forgotten just how big it was. I asked for some light and it spat out one of its glowing orbs. I tossed it just above my head. As I walked around the room, the orb followed my movement. The bed, the entire room, was a mess. The blankets and pillows had been tossed about, all the dresser drawers were open, some had their contents spilled on the floor. The place had been ransacked.

I opened the door and walked out into the hall, the bathroom to my right, the backdoor to my left, and the kitchen in front of me. I heard a noise coming from the other end of the trailer, so either the living room or my bedroom. On instinct alone, I plucked the glowing orb out of the air and stuffed it in the pocket of my hoodie. I crouched down and slowly crept the length of the hall until I was in the kitchen. The snake uncoiled and followed alongside me. From the corner of the kitchen, I could see half of the living room, the front door, and the door to my bedroom. The living room window was open, and a light pole just outside was on, so I could see the room well enough, though everything had a yellow tint.

The front door was shut but my bedroom door was wide open. The noise came from my room. I waited until a figure came out and into the light. I recognized him, though I had not ever properly met him. It was the person from the congregation who had their hand on the overseer's shoulder when Thread and Dust made their entrance. The person who opened that blackhole thing allowing the overseer to escape when Vrail started rampaging. I remembered back to exactly what had happened, it had looked like he had to touch a wall, or maybe just touch something, in order to open the hole or portal, whatever it was. Mentally I made a request to the snake for its help.

Faster than I thought something without legs would be capable of, the snake was across the kitchen and living room and wrapped around the man before me. The snake had followed my request and wrapped in such a way that the man's upper arms were pinned to his side, but his hands were held out in front, unable to move or touch anything. I stood up and walked into the living room, he on one side, me on the other. I didn't know exactly what he was capable of, so I wanted to keep my distance. If he was surprised to see me or surprised at being wrapped up by an anaconda in the middle of Lankon, it didn't show on his face.

I walked over to the curtain and pulled it shut, darkening the room. I slid the orb out of my pocket and tossed it high up in the middle of the room. At the closer distance, and with the illumination from the orb, I got a better look at him than I had in the congregation. His hair was brown and cut short. He was fit, very fit. Square jaw and hard, blue eyes. Frankly, he looked like he stepped off the pages of a comic book.

"What are you doing here?" It was the first thing I could think to ask.

He didn't speak, didn't answer, didn't move. He was just wrapped up and staring at me.

"Who are you?"

Still no reply.

I considered asking the snake to squeeze a little tighter, press some answers out of him, but before I could the snake's head reared back. It opened its mouth and sunk its teeth into his body. The man spasmed briefly and I almost released the snake, then I remembered that this man had watched me be nailed to a stake, and was very likely the one who had kidnapped me and Fin in the first place and taken us to the congregation. Suddenly, his mouth opened. He spoke in a robotic monotone.

"I'm looking for your mom, your brothers, or any clue as to where they are. My name is Greg."

It took a few seconds to realize he'd answered both of my questions. Though the snake had its teeth buried in his chest and stomach, he didn't seem to be in any pain. I started to think the snakes bite was compelling him to speak. Whether it compelled him to speak the truth or not, I didn't know.

"Who sent you?"

"The overseer."

Still a flat monotone with no change to his facial expression.

"Why do you... why does he want my family?"

It was a pointless question; I already knew the answer.

"To control you."

"Because he thinks I'm some sort of chosen one? Does he think I'm an answer to some stupid prophesy about raising God?"

"There is no chosen one and there are no prophesies in God's Own."

His flat voice was grating on my nerves.

"So, if I'm not some chosen one, why does he want me so badly?"

"You are just a tool to him, a means to an end. You and your abilities became known to the congregation, and the overseer has decided to use you to raise his God."

His God, he said *his* God, not our God, or my God.

"I know you have at least one ability. I watched you open that hole in the wall in the congregation and you and the overseer were sucked through. Why are you helping someone who is just using you for your ability?"

There was the slightest hesitation before he said," Void, not hole. Yours is not the only family in danger. He has my nephew, my only real family, and if I do not do what he commands, the overseer will kill him."

I needed time to think. I clearly am not great at processing new information on the spot. I needed time to plan my next steps. Initially, I had intended on having the snake kill this man, but after his confession I couldn't bring myself to do it.

I knew I was going to need extra help in order to keep myself safe while not killing this Greg person. When I was practicing my abilities in the field, I went to a great many other realms and I got to know a great many beings and their unique powers that I haven't specifically written about. I sat on the couch and pushed again. I made my way to a realm that was just an ice field. It was flat and bluish white as far as I could see. A few yards in front of me was a small mound. As I approached it, it was clearly a small igloo, just about two feet in height.

Out of it walked what I can only describe as a tiny, one-foot-high Yeti. Really, imagine the normal description of a Yeti, but reduce it to one-foot-high. He looked at me, and I swear he exhaled an irritated sigh. Back in the trailer, the tiny Yeti was between me and Greg, who was still wrapped in the snake. I looked at the Yeti and pointed at Greg. This time there wasn't just an obviously annoyed sigh, the little beast rolled his eyes at me too. I think that little guy has way more personality than I've seen from most of the other beings.

With some effort, he scaled up the snake, until he reached Greg's head. It was hard to see it unless you knew it was there, the way I did, but he had a little hammer strapped to his back. The head of the hammer looked as if it were made of ice, and given the realm he came from, it likely was. In one smooth motion he bopped Greg on the head. Greg was unconscious from the moment of impact. The little jerk had done the same thing to me in the field.

I looked from Greg's sleeping face to the tiny Yeti on his shoulder. He gave me a look that I can only interpret as 'well, are we done here, you asshole'? I released him.

Then I had the snake slowly uncurl from Greg and drop him gently to the floor. Once I was certain he was asleep I released the snake. Once released, the glowing orb disappeared, but I could see a bit better in the darkness than I could when I first entered the trailer. I walked into my bedroom. It was even more ransacked than mom's room had been. I grabbed the small stack of books that the librarian had given me. Then, I headed to the back door and left the trailer. I met Vrail back at the school where I had left her, and we headed back to the cabin.

Four

That all happened a few days ago and I have been hanging out at the cabin with Vrail, trying to decide what my next move should be. I considered spying on the overseer, the way I had tried to spy on Fin before I knew he could see me. If what Fin said is true, I could spy on the overseer and he wouldn't be able to see me. I stopped that line of consideration when I realized he must have access to others with abilities. There was no reason to believe it was just Greg and whoever this other person was who he used to control my mom. What if one of the others had some ability to see me? Would they be able to trap me? Until I understood more about all these different powers everyone seemed to have, I didn't want to take too large of a risk.

I really wanted to see my mom. I wanted to see if she was really with Fin, wherever he was. When I visited Fin, I just saw the one room and didn't think to ask where he was located.

I thought about spying on Thread or Dust, to find out if they were near Fin. I suspect he's with some group, but I don't have any information to guess at their size.

I considered spying on my brothers but given that I wasn't sure if they could see me or not, I didn't want to try it. I wasn't sure how much Fin, or anyone from Fin's group, had told them. Fin said they were all there, and that mom was unconscious, but he didn't really mention what they'd done with my brothers once they got them there.

I have to do something. I don't want to just sit here wasting more time. This evening I'm going to see my mom.

Five

Instead of going to bed I decided to lie down on the couch. Vrail couldn't fit upstairs and I wanted my body to stay within her sight. She knew my plan, so instead of curling up in front of the glowing fire, she sat at attention across from the couch, ready to be my defense if needed. I used The Healers breathing technique and settled my mind. I pushed to my mom, but my mom in that moment, not in the future.

I was in a brightly lit room and I was facing a wall. I looked down and I was in my suit with my comforting watch and fox pin. I turned and looked around. My eyes had to adjust to the oppressive brightness from all the overhead exposed lighting. A curtain was drawn in the middle of the room and I heard a man's voice on the other side. It wasn't Fin. I stepped past the curtain, unprepared for any of what I saw. Fin was in a chair next to a hospital type bed, holding my mom's limp hand. Next to Fin was the Dark Woman, just standing there, staring at my mom. I was so startled I yelped and fell backward onto my butt and hands. Fin jumped out of his seat and looked right at me. The other man looked around but clearly didn't see me and just went back to making notes on his clipboard.

In a flurry, the Dark Woman was on me, and I mean on me. I could feel her. Her speed wasn't human, and she had my shoulders in a vice. Then it wasn't my shoulders, she fully wrapped her arms around me and squeezed so tight I could hardly breath. I started to release my mind so I could get back to my body as quickly as possible, but Fin was right next to me. He yelled, told me not to go, not to be scared. He put one hand on my chest and one on the shoulder of the Dark Woman and gently pushed us apart. He could touch her, really touch her, like she had done to me.

My jaw was dropped. My eyes were watery. I was terrified. This woman had haunted my childhood. I don't know if I could vomit while in that other form of mine, but if I were going to, that would have been the moment. The Dark Woman stood at my feet. I was still on the ground, then Fin wrapped his arms around me, but not nearly as tightly as the nightmare woman had.

"It's OK, it's OK, you're fine, she isn't going to hurt you."

His voice was so calming, so full of feeling, I couldn't help but believe him.

"That's your mom."

I looked up at her, this vision of terror who had prompted my insomnia, given me countless nightmares, consumed my thoughts for so much of my childhood, and I really *looked* at her. I looked at the face behind the dark veil. The round cheeks, the short curly hair, the glasses, the turquoise earrings. It was my mom.

Fin helped me to my feet and I walked over to her. I stopped just inches in front of her. Her mouth moved, but I couldn't hear anything she said.

Fin said, "She doesn't have a voice in this state. She can hear us, but we can't hear her. We have no idea how to get her back in her body, we don't even know where to begin." His voice was choking up. I think he still cares for her.

By then, the man with the clipboard had left the room. It seems he couldn't see me, and couldn't see my mom, but he didn't seem at all shocked by Fin running around, reacting to and talking with ghosts.

"Have you tried, like, just laying her back inside her body?"

As I mentioned before, I always need time to process new information, otherwise I only comment on the obvious.

"She's tried that, I've watched her walk over to her body and try to grab it, but it's like something's over her body, keeping her from actually making contact."

Every word he formed was done so with a combination of warmth and sorrow, so different from the man who used to tell me about B horror movies.

For the first time since entering the room, I looked at my mom's body, flat on the bed. It wasn't just my mom, not exactly. The body was hers, but there was clearly someone else superimposed on her, like a double exposure in a photograph. They had a bitter smile. I couldn't tell for sure, but the features seemed to be those of a woman.

"Get that person out of her body first, then maybe she can get back in."

I'm sure I sounded like a real jerk, like I was so smart and there was no way they would have thought of that already.

I was still looking at her body when I said it. The bitter smile disappeared and was replaced by a look of rage. It was surreal. The face of my mom's body never changed, but the superimposed face was clearly angry.

"What are you talking about? What do you mean, someone else is in her body?"

Fin was looking from me to my mom's body, to my mom, then over again. My mom, the Dark Woman version of my mom, just stood there. She stared at her body with a sudden look of horror at the realization of why she couldn't get back inside. It was being occupied by someone else.

"I can see someone else in her, it's like their features are overlayed on hers. Not just her face, her whole body. Don't you see it? Don't either of you see it?"

As horrible as the thought of some other person in my mom's body was, I was hoping it was real and not me going crazy.

"I don't see anything but her body," Fin said. He looked over at my mom." Do you see anything?"

She shook her head from side to side, then thrust her hands at her body, just as fast as when she had run at me earlier.

It was a sight. Every time her fingers got close to her body there was an explosion of blue light that burst up, but I was the only one who could see it. The person in her body laughed. I couldn't hear it, but I could see it. They thought it was hysterical. Each grab she made at her body, the superimposed person wriggled a little, like they were repositioning themselves to keep hold. The Dark Woman would reach, the blue light would explode, the phantom in her body would reposition.

I stood next to her body and waited. As soon as I saw the other person's arm flip up enough, I grabbed it. As soon as I did, I knew that Fin and my mom could suddenly see this other person too. In my real body I'm the weakest person I know. But in my projected body, I always feel strong. I yanked as hard as I could, and the other person came flying out of Mom. As soon as they were out, they had a voice we could all hear. They screamed like a banshee. Not like the Glowing Woman, but like someone who is simultaneously terrified, shocked, angry, and humiliated. They jumped to their feet. It was definitely a woman, but none I recognized. They immediately began to run back to my mom's body.

In a flash the Dark Woman was between this other woman and the body lying on the bed. She punched her arm out and hit the woman square in the middle of her chest. The woman flew through the air and burst into bright blue shards as soon as her body hit the wall. The shards all fizzled and disappeared before they could hit the ground.

Before I knew what was happening, Fin was guiding the Dark Woman into mom's body.

It wasn't like the superimposed person. It was like the body of the Dark Woman inside the Victorian clothes just sank until its features were perfectly aligned with those of the body. The dress and veil just deteriorated into the bed and weren't there anymore. Her eyes opened and fluttered a bit. She tried to sit up but had trouble moving.

"It's your muscles, you haven't used them in so long, you…"

Fin's voice trailed off to tears. He lifted her upper body into his arms and wrapped her in a bear hug. With difficulty, she got her arms up and around him, but her eyes were on me.

"It wasn't me, I'm so sorry, it wasn't me and I couldn't stop it."

She was raspy, much more so than I'd ever heard her before. Fin grabbed a glass of water from a table next to the bed and brought it to her lips. She drank the entire glass.

"At first I thought it was a dream, I thought I was crazy. I'd lie down to go to sleep and suddenly I was out of my body, dressed like you saw me. It was fun, in the beginning. I would walk around while everyone slept. It started happening so much, I realized it was real. I thought I was special, that I was causing it to happen. Then it started happening when I was awake. I wasn't choosing to do it. I realized I was being pushed out. I was pushed far away, most of the time I didn't know where I was. Then, the more it happened, the more I fought it, the closer to my body I stayed. I saw what was happening. Even though I wasn't in my body, it was still being controlled. It did such horrible things. So horrible."

She looked at her own hands. She must have remembered what she watched those hands do to me. She hit herself with them, pounded them on her legs, so hard she was going to leave bruises.

Fin grabbed her wrists to stop her. He leaned in and whispered in her ear. She stopped fighting against his hold and they embraced again.

I knew I was seconds away from ugly crying and running to her, so I just released myself and was back in my body in a blink. As soon as I was back in the cabin, I realized what a jerk move that was, that they would both probably be angry with me for just disappearing like that without a word. I didn't care. I knew that if I stayed there, I was going to run up and hug her myself, but I didn't want my reunion with my real mom, her in her real body, to be with my other form. I wanted the real me to hold the real her.

Six

This morning, I remembered the overseer's words, about using a telepath to get information from my mom, then to control her, and then taking control completely. I knew it must have been the woman I pulled out of my mom's body. I also knew I needed to stop her before she tried to take control again.

The anger I felt toward her was so violent I wanted to kill her myself, slowly and painfully. I knew I couldn't do that. I wasn't strong enough, and I doubt I could have the stomach to do that kind of dirty work myself, but I had already proven I could plan someone's death, and watch, and enjoy it.

I visited a few of the other realms, trying to find the right being to help me. I thought about using Vrail, but the closeness I feel to her prevented it. I love that she defends me, but I don't want her to be part of a proactive murder. There's a difference to me, between killing to defend me, and killing for me.

As I travelled from realm to realm, my mind wandered. I thought about the phantom being in my mom, the Dark Woman version of my mom, Fin. I thought about how Fin, the Dark Woman, and I could see each other. I was in my projected form and my mom was in the Dark Woman form. It made a kind of sense, sort of, after what Fin had said. It made sense that I could see Mom outside of her body, and she could see me, and that Fin could see me, but I was getting stuck on how Fin could see the Dark Woman. They were not related by blood, so what let him see her?

I'll have to remember to ask him the next time I see him. Don't get me wrong, I know it isn't some incest thing. I'm sure the overseer would have flaunted that kind of info before he had me nailed to a stake. Maybe it's another passive ability of Fin's?

Also, I considered Mom's appearance as the Dark Woman. It was terrifying. Even knowing now that it was my mom, I still shudder when I think of the visual of her standing in my room that first time in California, or in the field just staring down at my body. Why the Victorian dress and veil? Just using some critical thinking, I wonder if it wasn't a choice. After all, my suit, tie, watch, and fox pin weren't some conscious choice. Maybe when we go outside of our bodies it's our subconscious that determines what our ideal appearance is. When I was young, very young, Mom used to watch PBS all the time for the British mysteries. A lot of them took place in Victorian times. Maybe she secretly wanted to live in that time.

One thought led to another. Had my mom, while in the form of the Dark Woman, watched what Hal had done to me? Had she watched what I'd had the Glowing Woman do to him?

I'm so tired of questions. Each time that I've thought I have answers, that I understand what's going on, the more I think about things, the more it all just leads to more questions.

I need a distraction. After I kill this woman, maybe Vrail and I will take a little vacation. I've always wanted to see Ireland.

I didn't think of any particular realm. I didn't control where I was going. I just turned my head and let chance take me from realm to realm. As I have clocked more experience over the past months, I've realized I don't need to bring the beings to my world to see their powers. I can ask them while in their realms. I wish I had known that before Big Green, though in retrospect that wasn't really that bad. No one died and only one house was destroyed as far as anyone knew.

I ended in a realm of yellow hills. I don't know what color the actual ground was, the yellow looked and felt like a type of moss growing on the ground. Many of the realms didn't have a smell, but that one smelled of cleanness. Like fresh laundry, far off flowers, trees. All I could see was bright yellow moss on hill after hill.

I felt calm there. It was a peaceful environment. I decided to walk around for a bit. After a few minutes I saw a white boulder, or puff of something, not too far away. As I made my way closer, it moved, which I expected. Once I was a few yards away I saw it wasn't as big as I thought it was from a distance. It was a mound that came up to my waist. I stood there and waited. Slowly some legs stretched out, and then a head, then it was standing there on all fours in front of me. It was a small white bear with eyes as yellow as the moss on the ground. It sniffed the air in my direction a few times, then sat down. I can't deny, it was so cute I wanted to run over and pet and hug it and call it a good boy. I refrained. These beings deserve my respect, and I know that.

Once that initial urge to cuddle him passed, I asked what he could do. He let out a tiny, squeaky, adorable, roar. Then a ball of lighting blew up near us. It was far enough away it didn't touch us in any way. It also didn't come from the sky. It wasn't a bolt. It was a ball that just blew up right there.

I thought about how cute it would be if the tiny Yeti rode on the little white bear's back into battle, if the tiny Yeti didn't act so put out all the time.

I called the bear back to the cabin with me.

As I sat up on the couch, the little bear walked over to Vrail and sat down next to her. It made a noise that's hard to explain. It was kind of like if a dog tried to purr like a cat. Vrail wrapped an arm around it and pulled it closer to her and nuzzled the side of her face against it.

I went upstairs and changed clothes. I changed into the dark pants and hoodie that I wear when I have Vrail take me somewhere people might see me. Once I made my way back downstairs, I knew that I could have Vrail take us, along with the little bear, to wherever the woman was. Instead of doing that, I wanted to spy a little first, mostly to make sure she was somewhere alone, and somewhere with enough space for me, Vrail, and the little bear to fit. I wanted us to show up right next to her, so she wouldn't have a chance to run or do anything to stop us.

I lay down on the couch again and pushed to her. I still had no idea who she was, but once she was out of my mom's body I got a good look at her, and I just brought that image of her to my mind when I pushed. I was hoping that the version of her in that form had the same face as her real body. When I projected, mine did, and as I found out it was still Mom's real face under the veil of the Dark Woman.

I was in a barn, a big barn. There were stalls all along the edges, I think for horses, but there weren't any animals in them. Not that I could see at least. The woman was at the opposite end, at a work bench. I walked over, hoping her ability wouldn't allow her to see me. I walked close enough to see there were no other people with her and then let myself go back to my body.

As I raised my head and opened my eyes, I heard Vrail purring and the little white bear squeaking. I looked over and they were play fighting in the living room. Vrail was so very much bigger, but they just took turns batting at each other and dancing around in a circle, posturing. They weren't really fighting, they were just having fun and messing with each other. I didn't want to interrupt, so I let them go at it for a few minutes. Then I started thinking that if I waited too long, the woman might not be in the barn any more.

After a few more moments, the two settled and looked over at me. They both sat, very properly. The little bear looked up at Vrail for approval. I explained to Vrail where I wanted to go, and I explained the overall plan. We would go to the barn, and if the woman was still in the barn, and still alone, I wanted the little bear to zap her before she had a chance to notice we were there. I don't know anything about telepaths, so I didn't want to leave any opportunity for her.

I walked over to where they were sitting. The little bear leaned into Vrail, and Vrail lowered her forehead to mine.

Vrail was perfect. We appeared just far enough from the workbench that the woman would not have had time to notice us before our attack, if she had still been alive. She wasn't. She was in pieces on the ground, at least eleven pieces at a quick count. Thread was leaning against one side of the workbench. Dust was leaning against the other side. Thread's voice was as deep and raspy as it had been the last time I saw her, in the congregation.

"We thought we might see you here."

Seven

The tiny bear looked from them to me, a question on his face. Thread raised her hands, palms out toward me.

"We aren't here to fight, don't think we could even if we wanted to."

Dust shot a look at Thread and shook her head a little.

"It's OK. He's Fin's kid, he'll find out soon enough anyway."

"Find out what?" I really wanted to have Vrail take us away, but Vrail looked perfectly at ease, so I assumed we were safe.

"Our abilities, we don't think they work on you, or on your friends."

I was glad she said friends instead of pets. Vrail might have taken her head off if she'd said that.

"What do you mean? And what exactly are your abilities?"

"I see these thin, white, glowing threads in the air. They wrap around everything. I can tug them, and when I do they cut right through anything I pull them through. Dust, my sister, she can turn any organic matter into sand. We can do a few other things too, but those are our main abilities."

Her voice was perfect. She should narrate audio books.

"And why don't you think your abilities work on me?"

"At the congregation, I noticed there weren't any threads around you. Then, when the big one here showed up and started tearing through people, I noticed there weren't any threads around them either. Right now there aren't any threads around any of you. And as for Dust, she doesn't see anything constant like I see the threads, but when she's ready to use her ability, she can tell what is organic and what isn't. If it's something her ability will work on, it takes a grayish hue. Not any of you though, so she doesn't think her ability will work on you either. So, like I said, we aren't here to fight you and even if we were, there's nothing we could do to you."

"Thank you for telling me that. At least, as long as you're telling the truth."

"Wow, I see you're just as trusting as Fin." Her left eyebrow cocked up as she smirked at me.

"How do you know Fin?"

Thread's smirk disappeared and her eyes momentarily looked lost.

"He helped us out of a very bad situation. We've stuck with him since then. He's a great guy, one of the few guys who doesn't expect something in return for his help."

I looked over at Dust.

"Does she talk? She was quiet at the congregation; she hasn't said anything now. Can she not talk?"

"She talks to me. She chooses not to talk to anyone else."

"What's this group you're part of? Is Fin in charge of it?"

I felt like I was pressing my luck by continuing to ask questions, but if it was true that they couldn't harm me, I wanted to press as much as I could.

"I wouldn't say we are part of them. We are there for Fin. He isn't in charge, there's a woman named Myrtle who runs the group. She's not so bad, kind of nice actually, and brilliant. We just aren't so much for joining groups where we have to let someone else make our decisions for us."

The sisters shared another look that I'm sure meant

something I didn't have enough context to understand.

"How did you know to come here? How did you know she would be here?"

That should probably have been my first question.

"Soon as you pulled her out of your mom's body, your mom and Fin could see her. Those two are connected through you. This is all new and we are all trying to figure things out as they develop, so we don't know how extensive the connection is or exactly how it works. Then there's the fact that your mom doesn't have any abilities, but Fin does, so we don't know how that plays into the connection either. Anyway, that's getting off track. As soon as Fin could see this woman, he recognized her. He's done more reconnaissance on God's Own than anyone. He had a contact he thought would know where she was, so we visited them. They directed us here. Her bits and pieces had just hit the ground when you showed up."

"Well, but then—," I began, but before I could finish my next question, Thread cut me off.

"Hold on, just slow down for a second. I am sure you're confused, and I'm sure you could continue asking questions for the next few hours. We've been in a similar position, so we really do understand, I'm not just saying that. However, we might not be the best two to answer your questions. That should probably be your dad, and maybe Myrtle. If you want to keep projecting yourself over, you can talk to Fin, ask him more questions. Before you do that, please consider seeing him in person. We know you're scared and being cautious. He would never say it, but we can see it's hurting him to know you don't trust him. There's no reason you should trust him, we get that. This is all so fresh for you, but Fin is the best of anyone we've met. And whether you realize it or not, you've been the center of his life since you were born. Throw him a bone, please."

Either she was extremely earnest, or she was an amazing actor.

"I don't know. I don't think it's Fin I don't trust. I don't know what you know, I don't know how much you know about my life, what I've been through. I don't have any reason to trust anyone. Everyone is a stranger, even Fin and my mom. How do I know someone in this group isn't really a member of God's Own and that they'll come for me?"

"I'm not saying to go to the group, I'm just asking you to consider seeing Fin as yourself, instead of a projection. He's important to us, and it would mean a lot to him. Take your buddies here if it makes you feel better about your safety. Take as many as you'd like. You don't have to go where they are. If you want to see Fin, just tell us where you want to meet him and we'll make sure he gets there. As far away from anyone else as you'd like. If you want, we could be there too, but if you don't want us to, it's fine. Just, if you want us to keep watch or anything, we can do that. We remember what it feels like, to learn about this stuff and not know what end is up."

I hoped everything she said was true, it would be nice to have friends who had been through what I've been through.

"Vrail hasn't ripped you apart yet, and the little one hasn't zapped you, so I guess they trust you. If they do, I guess I should too. For now at least."

I didn't mean to sound passive aggressive, but I wanted to be as honest as I was hoping they were.

"Vrail? They have names? That's interesting." Thread looked at Vrail like she admired her.

"She's my friend and I didn't want to call her Big Cat, so I named her Vrail-Thunne, but I just call her Vrail. I haven't named many of them. I don't know if they have names already. Maybe they do and it's insensitive of me to replace their names."

Vrail looked at me and purred.

"But I think she likes the name."

"Maybe she likes that you treat her like a friend and not a slave. Some people with power have a hard time doing that."

Each time she spoke, I wanted to know more about the sisters' past.

"Please, have Fin at the bleachers at the park in Lankon at six o'clock tomorrow evening. You can be there with him. Vrail will pick you up there. You'll each have to touch her. She'll bring you to where we're staying. Also, just so you aren't surprised, I'll have a lot of my friends at our place, just in case anything goes awry."

As if to make the point, the little bear made a trembling noise and the pieces of the woman lying on the ground blew up and away into a ball of electricity.

Eight

It has been two weeks since that conversation with Thread and Dust in the barn. They, along with Fin, have come over every evening since. The past few days, Fin has stayed at the cabin with me. There isn't enough sleeping space for four, so Vrail takes Thread and Dust back and then picks them up the following evening again. It's like we are developing a weird little family.

That first evening was not at all what I expected. I had pulled a dozen or so of my friends from the other realms. They were mostly hidden in the trees around the cabin, but a few were so large they couldn't hide. A few were inside, hiding in the rafters and shadows. I had planned on asking Thread and Dust to stay outside, to help my friends guard the area, and I had a huge list of questions I wanted to ask Fin.

As soon as I saw Fin in person, for the first time since the congregation, all the questions just went away. Before I had a moment to think about it, I had my arms around him, and his wrapped around me. Neither of us said anything. We just stood there, both silent, with tears running down our faces. I looked up and Thread and Dust were gently smiling, not smirking. I could almost see a sigh of relief in their eyes.

I invited them all to sit down and I made us some coffee. As I brought the coffee over, the room was full. Thread and Dust sat on the couch, Fin in a chair next to them, Vrail and Puff curled together in front of the fireplace, even though it was too warm to light a fire. Puff is what I decided to name the little bear. He's become a constant fixture alongside me as much as Vrail. I think Vrail really enjoys having the little guy around.

My chest felt unusual. It took a few minutes to figure out that it wasn't a physical issue, it was a feeling of contentment. There I was, in my cabin, with Vrail and Puff, my dad, and two new friends. I didn't feel in danger, I didn't feel like I was being manipulated or controlled, I didn't feel abused or hated.

I took the seat near the fireplace, next to Vrail and Puff. I pulled a little notepad out of my pocket and raised it up in front of me.

"Now that you're here, this feels silly to admit, but I wrote out a bunch of questions I wanted to ask you."

This received a huge bout of laughter from all three of them. I looked at all of them, not knowing what was so funny. Obviously something was funny to them, and the overreaction was a manifestation of the tension they must have been feeling being cut.

When their laughter subsided, Fin pulled a notebook out of his pocket and raised it up.

"I always keep this in my pocket. Every question I have and every answer I find, I write down. I also keep notes on everyone I meet in case I ever need to go back and reference anything."

The smile on his face was huge, from nowhere, we suddenly had this common thing between us.

I jumped out of my chair and ran upstairs. I grabbed this journal and brought it downstairs.

"I've been writing down everything! The notepad in my pocket is for questions and general thoughts on what I should do next, but I started this journal after the congregation kidnapped both of us. After we escaped, I wanted to write down everything while it was fresh in my mind. I went back to the first memory I had of anything unusual happening to me."

The jaws of Thread and Dust dropped, and if it were possible, Fin's smile grew even bigger.

"You're a writer! Do you remember that first time you projected to my room? All those books on the shelves, those are the journals I've been keeping since all this started!"

I know it's such a small thing, but this shared thing we both do, that we didn't know the other did, it felt monumental. It was more than words, it felt like proof he really is my dad, like writing is an inherited trait I received from him. What I wouldn't give to read his journals. I saw his eyes on my journal and guessed he felt the same way.

"I've almost stopped writing a few times. Initially I started my journal so I could get my facts straight, try and remember details I hadn't thought about in a long time, and look for clues about what was happening to me. Now, it's become a place to list questions and give short updates. I don't really know for who though, I hadn't really thought about letting anyone other than me read it. I think it would have been easier to write my story from a different perspective. Writing from my own makes it so personal, it was difficult to get through a few of the entries. I've been a little weird about it too. Like, I wrote the entire first part, from the first time I could remember something strange happening through God's Own kidnapping us, in one sitting. It was a blur, getting it all down. I'm terrible with dates, so even though it's my journal I couldn't add specific dates for the entries. Then, when I got caught up to real time, I still didn't add dates because I wanted to keep with the format I started in."

I had been looking at the journal in my hands.

"When you wrote it, did it help ease your mind? Mine did for me. It was cathartic, a way of facing everything I had been through, acknowledging it was real, and planning my next steps. And if you want to try a different style, then do it. It's your journal, there's no wrong way to go about it. You can try second or third perspective or use an omniscient narrator. I pepper my journals with bursts of omniscient narration when it's in more exciting parts. And who cares about dates, it's the story that matters."

"Yeah, it did help ease my mind. And it definitely helps me plan, it helps me remember the little details."

I set it on a bookcase near my chair. We spent the rest of the evening, and into the night, just talking, Fin, Thread, and I, while Dust's interactions came largely from very animated facial expressions and gestures. We didn't talk about the questions I'd written down, or the ones Fin had written down either. We just talked about nothing really. All three of them love to read so we perused through the ample collections I had in the cabin. We compared suggestions, likes, and dislikes. Fin picked out a few of his favorite epic fantasy books that I hadn't read and made a little stack for me on an end table. Thread said she and Dust love horror books but that they had never actually been able to do much reading since it wasn't easy to get to a library. I picked out half a dozen of my favorites and gave them to the twins.

We talked about movies, or I listened as they talked. Fin was just as animated about them as he was back in the convenience store. The passion he showed for movies back then was clearly authentic. He talked about ones that had been adapted from books that he loved, and others he felt had ruined the story with a bad interpretation. He told me that when he was young, all he wanted was to be a writer, to tell a story original and great enough to be made into a movie. His two loves would come together, writing and movies.

"I've never really thought about writing like that. I've always read. It was my escape from everything at home, before I knew I could literally escape. I'd open a book and disappear into it, like I was really in the story. Hours, sometimes an entire day, would pass before I'd come back to reality. Other than school assignments, I didn't start writing until this journal, though I suppose it would make a good story for some people."

Fin looked like he'd been hit in the gut. I instantly regretted bringing up the need to escape from my life. I thought he must feel guilty for not being able to be there.

"I'm so sorry, I didn't mean to bring down the mood, I was just saying that reading is very important to me, it really helped me when I didn't have others to rely on." I wasn't sure if that would make it worse, or better.

"No. No, it's OK. It's just that, what you said, about reading as an escape before you knew you could literally escape. I had a friend, he said nearly those same words to me. Sorry, it just made me think about him. I really miss him. I think you and he would have been really good friends. You have a lot in common."

Thread and Dust both looked down at their laps. I got the feeling something awkward was going on, but I couldn't put my finger on it.

I wanted to know more, but I also didn't want to create a depressing atmosphere after having such an enjoyable time up to that point, so I said we should all go for a walk outside. It was dark, so I called down the snake. Fin, Thread, and Dust all jumped up as the giant anaconda uncoiled and dropped down from the rafters. They really had not noticed it up there, watching them the entire time. They were even more surprised when it coughed out a glowing orb that I could grab and toss around. Vrail got up and did some very cat like stretches, then Puff got up and tried to imitate those same stretches, making a chippy little noise the entire time.

We all walked in pairs outside, Fin and me in front, Thread and Dust in the middle, then Vrail and Puff at the end of our little troop. The paths around the cabin were big enough that we could have all walked together, but it felt very organic and OK to pair the way we did. None of us talked much, other than to point out the occasional interesting tree or plant that we saw. Some of the beings I had brought over were very obvious and easy to see. Others weren't, so I pointed a few out. At one point, as I explained the realm one of them came from and what it could do, Fin clapped his hand on my upper back, then rested it around my shoulders. I looked up at his face. He was clearly proud, proud of me. I could have teared up again, but I just smiled. I don't think anyone had ever been proud of me before Fin.

From out behind a shrub, the little Yeti popped up. He looked at me and Fin, rolled his eyes at us and gave a little sarcastic head shake, but it also looked like he had a tiny smile he was trying to hide. He walked right over to Puff and started scratching his front haunches. To compare the size of the two, the little Yeti is about as big to Puff as I am to Vrail. My heart jumped, because I thought it might be what I'd hoped for, that the little guy would ride Puff. It didn't happen, he just scratched away, then followed along as we continued to walk. I did start to wonder if all of the other beings adored Puff the way Vrail and now the little Yeti did. I knew I needed to name the little Yeti, but it was difficult, because I didn't want to offend him, and he did seem to take offense easily. I pondered on it the rest of the walk. As we neared our way back to the cabin, I had a different idea.

"Thread, if you two had to name this little guy," I said, and pointed to the little Yeti. "What would you name him?"

He looked from me to Thread, then crossed his arms and cocked an eyebrow as his gaze stayed on Thread.

"Us?" She looked at Dust. "You want us to give him a name?" I could hear the excitement in her voice.

"Yes. I've been trying to think of one for him, but I can't come up with anything. So, why don't you have a try?"

They both walked over to him and knelt down, still towering over him, but closer to his level. His little, tiny foot was tapping up and down as if he was telling them to get on with it. They whispered between each other, but I couldn't hear exactly what they were saying.

"Well, where we are from, there are sightings of Bigfoot, but the word we use is *waterbobbejan*. It translates to 'water baboon'. So, how about we call him 'Boon'?"

All our eyes were on him. He uncrossed his arms and cocked one shoulder up and his head down toward it and made a little *hmpff* noise, as if to say, "Fine," then went back to scratching Puff.

"Boon it is. Thanks!"

Now if he decides he doesn't like the name, he can't blame me for giving it to him.

Shortly after that we said our goodbyes and Vrail took them back to the bleachers by the field in Lankon.

The next evening they came back. Thread and Dust spent more time walking around outside. They mentioned that they didn't get to walk around in the woods very often, so they wanted to use the opportunity while they had it. It gave Fin and I time to talk alone, so I didn't mind them hanging around outside.

We pulled the two chairs together so they faced each other with a small table in between them. Fin brought a chessboard because I mentioned the night before that I really wanted to learn how to play. While we played, I asked some of my questions.

"How did you find out about your ability?"

I knew I was really asking him how he died the first time, but I did want to know when his ability manifested.

"It wasn't until after your mom left with you. I told you before that I was homeless for a stretch of time. I stopped showing up to work so I could go looking for you myself, so I lost my job. I'd used up all of my money trying to find you. I lost everything. I thought maybe she went to St. Louis to disappear. She used to talk about wanting to move there. She'd seen it in an old movie and fell in love with what she saw. It took almost a week, but between walking and hitchhiking I made my way there. That very first night, I slept behind a dumpster in an alley. I woke up in the middle of the night to someone holding a knife to my throat and going through my pockets. I reached up to push him, and he pulled his arm back and stabbed me in the throat. The blade was sharp. I don't remember feeling it going through. I do remember sitting there, him holding me down, me drowning in my own blood. Then I was kneeling over my own body, gripping the knife jammed in my throat. I thought it must be a nightmare. I didn't sleep for a few days after that, probably the shock of it all. I went back to that alley a few times to check on my body, make sure it was still there and actually me. Eventually it was found, I guess, because it was gone the last time I went to check on it."

It was a horrible story. I didn't really know how to react to it. If it weren't for his ability, he would have died that night. I would never have known him. The what ifs started to branch out in my mind. I tried to stay focused, on the conversation and our chess game. "

How many times has it happened?"

He considered his next move, and didn't answer until after he had moved the piece that looks like a little castle tower halfway up the board.

"A few dozen, over the years."

"Why didn't God's Own know what you can do?"

His eyebrow cocked up and his head tilted a bit as he looked at me.

"In the congregation, if they had known what you could do, the overseer wouldn't have told that guy to kill you. He would have known it would just free you from the restraints and give you a knife."

His eyebrow lowered and a half smile tugged the edge of his mouth upward. His eyes were back on the board. "You're observant. You picked up on that even in that horrible situation. I hope you realize how amazing you are, Hez. I've managed to keep it from them all these years. When I found out about them, I spied when I could. The more I understood about my ability, I felt safe with it. I may deal with the pain of dying, but I come back to do it all over again. When I would get into one of their locations, usually looking for files I could use to track you down, if I were ever found out, I'd just make sure the person who found me, killed me. No witnesses, and they weren't any the wiser about what I could do."

"But what about all the bodies? If there are a few dozen of your corpses lying around, won't the police think something is up?"

I assume that if the police had information like that, it would quickly make its way to God's Own.

"I got rid of them all. I had help with that."

He didn't give any further explanation.

"Now that they know though, it's going to be dangerous for

you. If they take you again, they'll know not to kill you. Or maybe they'll use on you whatever it was they used on me. It stopped my power from working."

I felt panicked. I was just getting used to the idea of having a dad, and here my mind was spiraling on losing him.

"I don't think it would work on me. From what we've found out about what they used on you it didn't actually hinder your ability. It just made it difficult for you to think and concentrate. You have to think about, and concentrate on, using your abilities to actively use them. Mine doesn't work like that. It just takes over when it needs to. But, you're right, things will be more dangerous for me now that they know. They could just keep me locked up. Maybe if they find some other way of killing me that doesn't involve someone specifically murdering me, like starving me, I won't come back. There isn't really a way of knowing until it happens."

I could tell he'd thought about this already.

"Let's talk about something lighter. How did you get back on your feet?"

He had mentioned that first time I visited him in his room that he ended up working for a newspaper in St. Louis, but I didn't know how he went from homeless and penniless to having a job.

He spoke while he pondered his next move.

"Well, after I wandered around St. Louis for a bit, numb and confused, I started to make a plan. I knew I needed one or I'd never find you. I found a shelter where I could get some sleep and shower. When I lost my home, I lost most of my stuff, but I did have a bag of clothes. Mostly just jeans and t-shirts, but I'd grabbed one suit. I applied for every job I was qualified for, every day started with me looking through trashcans finding discarded newspapers so I could check the help wanted sections. I knew no one would hire me if I used the shelter as my home address. I couldn't afford to rent a P.O. box, and even if I could, most employers would still want the home address too.

At the time, there were a lot of abandoned neighborhoods in St. Louis. So, I found one that seemed empty, picked a house, and started using it as my home address. I didn't actually stay there, or squat or anything. I just used the address on my applications. I went there every week or so to check the mailbox in case any of the places I'd applied with sent something."

He moved one of his horse pieces in an L pattern.

"I got lucky. It took a few months, but I was hired on at a small newspaper company in downtown. I'd love to say I was a reporter, but with no portfolio of work I didn't qualify for that. They put me to work with the printing press. Just maintenance and cleaning. It took time, but I saved up my money and found a cheap apartment that was walking distance to the paper company. And that's that. Checkmate."

I'd learned more about Fin, and learned I was not a chess prodigy.

We talked a bit more, not about anything serious, then went out for a stroll to meet up with Thread and Dust. Vrail took them back and I tried to get some sleep. It was difficult. I kept picturing Fin in that alley, being murdered. When I did get to sleep, it was just the same nightmare over and over. Fin, in the alley, stabbed. He didn't come back. He was dead. Just dead. Those dark eyes, lifeless and empty.

Spending our evenings like this has gone on for a few weeks. I still haven't won a game of chess, but I do know how to move each piece. Like some of us, they each have special abilities. I've also learned that the pawns are much more useful and important than I initially thought they were.

It was a few days ago that Fin started staying the night. He joined me in going to get water to bring back to the cabin. We go on hikes. We don't always talk. There is so much more I want to know about him, like how did he met up with this group that opposes God's Own? What did he do to help Thread and Dust that made them appreciate him the way they do?

Before I go on pressing him for more information, I thought I'd give him a chance to ask me questions. Then I had a different thought. *This journal holds everything he'd want to know about me, what I've been through and learned. I'm just going to give it to him to read, then if he has questions after that, he can ask all he'd like. Right now he's lying on the couch, reading a book, and I'm in my chair just finishing this entry.*

Now I'm just procrastinating, because I told him as soon as I'm done writing this, I'm handing it to him and going to bed. I wasn't keeping this journal with the expectation that my dad would read it one day, so now I'm trying to think back to everything I've written, and whether I wrote anything I don't want him to know about. I guess, at this point, he probably knows most of it anyway. So, here goes, just finishing this sentence and then giving it to Fin.

Nine

I woke up this morning to find Fin pacing back and forth downstairs. Vrail eyed him from a corner and flipped her tail hard on the ground. Puff just sat there and looked up at her.

"I keep asking Vrail to take me back, but she's just sitting there. I need to go back, please tell her to take me. Now. It's important."

He spoke quickly. I thought maybe he'd read something in my journal that made him mad.

"Did I do something? Why do you want to leave? We haven't even talked about my journal yet."

I wasn't ready for him to leave. I wanted more time with him.

"No, no, it's not that. It's what you wrote, when you went back to your trailer. Greg. I have to tell them about Greg."

His eyes watered.

"What about him? I didn't kill him. It sounded like he didn't want to be with God's Own, but they'd kidnapped his nephew. They were forcing him to help them."

I had written all of that down, so he must have known.

"No, you don't understand. You don't know everything that's happened yet. Greg was one of us. We were close. Remember that first night I came here, I said you sounded like someone I used to know? When you were talking about using books as an escape before you knew you could literally escape, you sounded just like him. He disappeared over a year ago. We didn't know what happened to him. He and I were partners, we did everything together. We were the ones accumulating all the information on God's Own. Then, he was just gone. After a week or two, everyone assumed he was dead. I told them we needed to keep looking, but they didn't want to waste more resources. Then, at the congregation, he was there. Nearly everyone, except me, thought he had turned, that he joined God's Own. I knew it couldn't be. He would never do that. Now it makes sense, he's being forced to help them or they'll kill Lincoln, his nephew. I have to go back. I have to tell them. We have to help him."

He was hurting but trying to keep it together. Dammit, why didn't I give him my journal to read earlier?

"Vrail, please send him, but you stay here and wait by my side. Puff, don't go with them. Stay here with me. Fin, Vrail will send you. As soon as you leave, I'm going to project to you. From what you've said, none of them will see me. This way, I'll know what's going on and how I can help."

I was hoping Mom wasn't there at the moment. I wasn't ready to see her again yet.

"Thank you. I'll see you there, son."

Vrail walked over to him, then Fin was gone.

I lay down on the couch and projected immediately. I just thought of Fin, and I was by his side in a big flat field. Vrail and Puff were by my real body in the cabin. Fin nodded to me, then reached down to the ground and lifted a door I would never have found. It was camouflaged with dirt and weeds. I went down the steps first, with Fin behind me so he could close the door. The steps led to a long hallway. The walls, floor, and ceiling all looked like concrete or cinder blocks. The light was low so it was hard to tell for sure. At the end of the hall was a large metal door with a keypad on it. Fin punched in some numbers and I heard a metallic thump. He grabbed a curved handle and pulled the door open. I slipped through, and he followed behind and closed the door. He pressed a button and I heard the metallic thump again, locking the door.

We were in a large room with a lot of rectangle tables that were all surrounded by chairs. There were people sitting at some of them eating. The tables weren't even close to being full, and only a few heads looked up when they saw Fin enter. He didn't stop to speak with any of them. Determinedly, he walked to another door on the opposite side of the room. The space beyond that door kind of looked like a hotel, with intersecting hallways and lots of doors that I guessed led to individual living quarters. The vibe was nothing like a hotel. It was more like an end of the world, underground bunker, cement, and exposed pipes type of vibe. After a few turns down various hallways, we came to a wall that had only one door. We stepped through. It was not at all what I expected.

The room had many desks with computers at each. There was a person at each of the desks, typing away. They all had headsets on, those kinds with the earpieces and little microphone that hangs down in front of the mouth. There were large monitors on the walls. Some of the monitors displayed maps, others seemed to show various files and information on them. There was a smaller room in a back corner, with glass walls and a round table inside. At the table I could see an older woman gesture emphatically, and a handful of other people watching her. We walked over and entered the room.

"Fin, it's good to see you. I didn't expect you back so soon, I thought you'd take some more time to spend with your son."

She smiled at him. She had a warm and kind voice.

"Myrtle, it's Greg. Hez saw him, he knows why Greg was

with the overseer. They have his nephew, they have Lincoln. They threatened to kill him if Greg didn't help them."

So that was Myrtle. Thread had mentioned her before.

"Is he sure? How would he know that?"

"Hez saw him when he went to the trailer looking for his mom and brothers. Greg was there, the overseer sent him to find clues. Hez had one of his friends there, they got the truth out of him. They have Lincoln, we have to help them both." Fin's words rushed.

"Fin, I understand what Greg means to you, and I'm glad we have this information. It means Greg didn't betray us, at least not willingly. Though it doesn't change much, does it? We don't have the resources to find them, much less help them. Greg was how we got everywhere. Without him, we are working within an extremely limited range of activity. You know that." She sounded apologetic. "I wish we had a way. We would all like to see Greg safe and back with us."

I knew they couldn't hear me, so when I spoke, it was just to Fin.

"I can help. I can project and find them, like I did with that lady in the barn who Thread killed. Then, Vrail can take us there to get them."

While I spoke, Fin continued looking at Myrtle. "I can talk to Hez, with his abilities, we could find Greg and Lincoln, bring them both here," he said.

Myrtle hesitated to respond, for just a moment. She looked like a worried grandmother.

"You and Hezekiah have both been through so much. Are you sure you want to put him, and you, in that kind of danger so quickly? We could try to find more information first, see if we can develop a plan that wouldn't require your son to be in that situation. He's so young, and he doesn't fully understand our world. He probably doesn't fully understand his abilities yet either, and, if he doesn't fully understand them, he can't fully control them. It's a very dangerous thing you're asking. What if he misunderstands something he sees, and you both end up captured again? With what they know about you now, we don't know what would happen."

At that point, Thread and Dust burst into the room. They must have heard Fin was back. They smiled at first, but when they saw the dark expression on Fin's face, their smiles quickly turned to concern.

"What's wrong?"

"It's Greg. He didn't betray us. God's Own found and took his nephew. They threatened to kill him if Greg didn't help them. Hez found out. I just learned about it last night. With Hez's help, we can find them both and save them."

Fin's voice was rocky. I realized he cared for Greg more than I initially thought.

"Well let's go then, what are we waiting for? Do you have a way of contacting Hez? Can he come get us now?"

Of course Thread and Dust were ready to help Fin.

Myrtle said, "Thread, Dust, in light of this news, of course we all want to help Greg. Right now, as we are stretched so thin, we should look for more information first. Try to confirm what Hez claims to know. Then plan accordingly, in a more thoughtful way than endangering Fin's son, and anyone else involved, by putting them in an uninformed and uncontrolled situation."

She was starting to sound stressed.

"With all due respect, Myrtle, you haven't seen what Hez can do. In the short amount of time we've known him, it's clear he's as thoughtful and tactical as Fin, he's as cautious as you, and he's far, far, more powerful than any of us. If anyone were going to successfully storm a God's Own stronghold, it's him."

Thread and Dust did not know I was there, so Thread wasn't saying that to blow smoke up my butt. She meant it. I made a mental note of that. After all, it's one thing to stand up for someone while they're in the room. It's another thing altogether to do so when they aren't.

"I appreciate your belief in him, but it took one needle to stop Hez from using his powers. What's to stop that from happening again?"

That had not crossed my mind until Myrtle said it.

Fin said, "First off, he and I both were taken by surprise that day. Also, he didn't have a team then. This time, he will, and we will know what to expect."

"I'm sorry Fin, I can't approve this. We need more time, more information."

Myrtle dismissed him and turned back to the others at the table.

Immediately I called mentally to Vrail. The next second she was there in the room. Most of those people sitting at the round table fell out of their chairs, others jumped up and pressed against the wall farthest from Vrail.

Fin looked at me and said, "Thank you, Hez." Then he, Thread, and Dust all reached up to touch Vrail and appeared back at the cabin. I let go of my projected form and rose off the couch back in my body.

"Well, where do we start?" I asked.

Fin grabbed my shoulders and drew me in to a hug.

"Thank you Hez. You can't understand how important this is to me. Thank you."

I looked up at Thread and Dust. They both gave one nod at

me.

"Sure, I'll do whatever you need me to do. So, what do you need me to do?"

Fin let go and started to come up with a plan.

"In your journal, it sounds like you don't have to know a specific place to project to it. You can just think about a person, or a thing, maybe even just an idea, and then you go where you're supposed to go. Does that seem correct?"

He was really paying attention when he read my journal.

"Yeah, that seems to be how it works. I can either push to a location or push to the future."

"Great, you'll need to do both for this to work. We need to know where Greg is, where Lincoln is, and what's going to happen when we go to get them both. Then we can plan which of your friends will be able to help us. Can you do that?"

He held my shoulders again. The hope in his eyes was obvious.

"Of course he can, he's the toughest person in the room. Isn't that right, Hez?" Thread has a knack for saying the right thing at the right time.

I smiled, then said, "I can start right now."

And so I did.

Ten

I spent the rest of yesterday on the couch, projecting to Greg, Lincoln, and slightly in the future to see as best I could how events would to unfold. Projecting to the future is what I'm least experienced at. I couldn't see exactly how things would turn out, and that worried me. I saw certain events, specific things that would happen that we would be prepared for, but I couldn't see whether our efforts would be successful or not. I knew there were things I was missing, but I spent as much time as possible gathering as many details as I could, to bring back to our small group at the cabin. I spent yesterday evening explaining everything to Fin, Thread, and Dust. We all agreed to take a night's rest to think about it and come up with a plan in the morning. Thread and Dust did not want to go back to the compound, so Vrail and I left to get them a tent and camping supplies, like an air mattress, sleeping bags, and pillows, as well as some clothes to sleep in. They had been wearing their tactical gear, the same outfits they had on the first time I met them in the congregation and had no other clothes with them. I had offered to get another bed to bring inside, but they seemed excited at the prospect of camping outside. Since Fin had already been staying at the cabin with me, he had extra clothes and his tactical outfit. When I projected to the future, I saw him in it. It was similar to the outfits Thread and Dust wore, but instead of being gray with black trimmings, his was dark-blue with green trimmings. His outfit also came with two guns, one holstered on each thigh, and two fighting sticks strapped to his back. I have to say, he looked like a badass.

This morning we reviewed through the notes Fin made last night. While I talked, trying to remember the details of what I had seen, he wrote them down. We formed our plan in less than an hour. The short of it was that Vrail would take the four of us to just outside of the location where they were keeping Greg. It was a large farmhouse in Pocahontas, Iowa, near Lankon. Thread, Dust, and Vrail would stay there, but Vrail would send Fin and I to another house that I believe was in Georgia. That's where Lincoln was being held. He was in a special room. If the pressure in the room changed suddenly, a collar that was around Lincoln's neck would send spikes through his throat. It would be a quick death. We figured they set things up this way in case Greg were ever to find out where Lincoln was being held. If he opened a void into the room, the pressure would change, and Lincoln would be killed.

The idea was that Fin and I would deactivate the room and get Lincoln out of the house. I would call Vrail, who would come get the three of us and take us to the place Greg was at and we would meet back up with Thread and Dust. After that, we would all go inside to get Greg. Greg would see Lincoln was safe, then we would all leave and go to the cabin. Along the way, I was ready to call on a few of my friends to help us out of some jams. Even after agreeing to the plan, I was nervous because I couldn't give anyone certainty of how things would end. It was like I could see up to a certain point, but at that point, I couldn't see anything further. My biggest concern was that it was a bad point and I didn't know if we would get out of it. We had to go forward anyway. Fin needed us to. I didn't know why Greg was so important to him, but he was, so he was important to me.

It took me a few minutes to jump from realm to realm to ask for the help we would need. As I had learned from the Glowing Woman, I could ask for help early and have them show up later when they were needed. It all didn't have to happen in the moment. When I was back in the cabin, the three others were standing there in their tactical outfits, waiting. I looked out of place, in my dark jeans and hoodie. I'm sure I looked even more out of place when I slid to the ground and started playing with Puff. He was coming with us, and I was worried about him. The point I couldn't see past in the future involved him.

"Before we go," Fin said. "I want to thank all of you. You don't have to do this, and I know Myrtle doesn't want us doing this, so I don't know how welcome we will be, back with the group, after we are done with this mission."

"We've never been part of the group. We were only there to support you," Thread said very decisively.

"I don't even know what the group is, like, do they have a name? You know, God's Own is called God's Own, but I've only ever called your people 'the group'. Like Thread said, we support you," was my contribution.

"They intentionally don't have a name." Thread rolled her eyes and went on. "They think anonymity gives them an advantage. It's nonsense. The Group has become a name of sorts, though if you tell them they are called The Group, they get their underpants in a wad about it."

Fin giggled at that.

"Just, thanks, OK. I know none of you have to do this, so, just thanks."

With that, we were off. The land around the farmhouse was hilly and unkempt. Vrail brought us to the side of a hill opposite the side the house was on, so if they had lookouts, they wouldn't see us. The main reason we left Thread and Dust there was so that they could give some advanced warning if it looked like any excitement was going on in the house with Greg while Fin and I got Lincoln. The tactical suits had communicators in them, so Fin would be able to stay in touch with them. We left Vrail there because of her size. We didn't want her to show up at the house with Lincoln until we were ready to exit. Puff stayed with them as well. We didn't need him to get Lincoln.

I've said before, I spent a lot of time going from realm to realm, in fact I still run through different realms most nights before I go to sleep, but I haven't written about many of the beings I met. For this mission, we needed several I haven't introduced yet. One of those, I call Shroud. She's sort of like a medium-sized black cricket. What she does is extremely helpful for spying. I wish I had known about her back when I was using Vrail to take me places to get money and supplies to live at the cabin. She can jump in my pocket and then let me be invisible. I had Shroud get in my pocket and I took Fin by the hand. The invisibility extended to him as well. Then we touched Vrail and she sent us to the hall outside the room Lincoln was being kept in.

Deactivating the room and collar was entirely on Fin. I know nothing about that kind of thing. He quickly had a panel dislodged from the wall by the door and fiddled with the wires. He pulled some little contraption out of a belt pack and clipped it onto some of the wires he'd pulled together. When he was about halfway through what he was doing, the Glowing Woman appeared next to me, right on time. I arranged it because I knew in just a few seconds half a dozen armed men were going to come running around the corner. Though the guards couldn't see us in their cameras, they could see the wall panel drop and wires move around.

As they all came into sight, she screamed directly at them. In an instant, they dropped their weapons and flung their hands up and over their ears. They were on their knees as she floated closer and closer to them. When she was feet from them, the scream intensified and her glow encompassed them all. When she quieted, they were all on the ground, dead. She raised her hand to them and there was a flash of blinding light. They were all gone, the weapons were still on the ground. I had been holding my hand on Fin's back to keep him invisible, but at that point I let go and walked over to the guns. I nodded at the Glowing Woman as I bent down to pick up a gun and she left, back to her own realm. At that point I walked over to the other end of the hall, knowing that another group was coming from that end. I picked up a particular gun. I don't know what to call it. It kind of looked like a shotgun, but it had this thing on top that launched grenades. I stood in the hall but raised the gun around the corner and blindly launched the grenade. There were screams, followed by a devastating explosion. I looked around the corner and saw only body parts and blood plastered on the walls. No whole people were left. We didn't need Shroud anymore, so I released her.

The whole thing took less than a minute. The Glowing Woman and I had collectively killed around a dozen men. I wondered if I should feel bad about that. In truth, I didn't really feel anything other than a desire to keep going and help Fin save his friend.

"Ready!" Fin called from the panel he was messing with.

I ran back over to him right as the door to Lincoln's room slid open with a hiss. Lincoln screamed and grabbed his collar, thinking it was going to go off when the door opened so suddenly.

Instead, Fin pressed another button on the panel and the collar fell to the ground.

"Lincoln, I know we never met, so you don't know me, but my name is Fin. I'm a friend of your Uncle Greg's. We are here to get you out and take you to him."

Fin spoke quietly, but clearly, not wanting to frighten the boy.

Before I had projected forward, I had expected someone older, someone closer to my age. He was so young. He looked maybe four years old, five at the most. God's Own had kidnapped an actual little child and threatened to kill him to get what they wanted. My hatred for the overseer grew a bit more.

"My uncle's here?"

Lincoln wasn't crying. At his age, I would have been bawling.

"No, he isn't, but we are going to take you to him right now. Is that OK?"

Apparently, Fin is good with children.

"OK. I want to see my uncle. They told me I'd never see him again."

Lincoln's voice started to warble, but he still didn't cry.

Fin and I walked over toward him. Fin said," Now, in just a few seconds, you're going to see something that might seem scary, but it really isn't. This is my son, Hezekiah. You can call him Hez."

I smiled and waved at Lincoln.

"He has some special friends who are going to help us. One of them is a giant cat with a long snout. She might look scary at first, but she's the sweetest giant cat you're ever going to meet. Her name is Vrail. She's going to take us to your uncle. Are you ready to meet her?"

This all made me wish even more that Fin had been there for me when I was Lincoln's age.

"Yes please." Lincoln has manners.

Fin radioed to Thread and Dust to let them know we were moving on to the next part of the mission and that we'd be with them momentarily. At the same time, I called Vrail, who appeared in the room with us. Lincoln's eyes became saucers, but just for a second. He ran right over to her with his arms out to pet Vrail

"Kitty! I love you kitty!"

He had one arm wrapped around one of her legs and with the other was petting her as high on her leg as he could reach. She looked from him to me to him to me and decided to tolerate it for the moment.

Fin and I walked over to her and each put a hand on her, Fin also put a hand on Lincoln's back, in case teleporting with Vrail for the first time was disorienting for him. Lincoln had his eyes closed as he squeezed Vrail. When he opened them again, we were at the hill with Thread, Dust, and Puff. He seemed unfazed by the mode of travel, and his eyes went straight to Puff. Lincoln made a little hitching noise and looked up at Fin.

"That's Puff, he's friendly too," Fin said. Lincoln ran just as quickly to Puff as he had to Vrail, wrapping his arms around him. They both rolled around on the ground, Lincoln laughing and Puff making his playful chittering noises.

"I... I didn't expect him to be so young."

Thread's voice was shaking. I think it made her as angry as it had made me. God's Own had been fucking with my life since I was born. The thought of them doing that to other children made my veins burn. Thread has said she and Dust knew what I was going through. I wonder if they'd been on the receiving end of God's Own attention at as young an age as I had been.

"I didn't know how young he was either. I didn't even know he had a nephew until a few years ago. You know, Greg, how he grew up, he didn't talk about family. I found him crying in his room one day. He said his sister and brother-in-law had been killed in an accident and that his nephew was being sent to a foster home." Fin spoke low so Lincoln wouldn't hear. "He wanted Lincoln with him, but he knew his life was too dangerous to bring a child into it."

I wonder if that was why Fin hadn't come for me. He had obviously planted himself at that convenience store between the trailer park and the post office. He knew who I was. He never said anything. Did he think his life was more dangerous than the life I was already living?

"I'm sorry," I spoke up. "When I pushed forward and saw him, I realized how young he was and I was shocked and angry, but I thought you all knew him, so I didn't bring it up."

I sounded a bit dazed, but that's because I was still thinking about Fin not taking me away from the life, I had been trapped in. As always, once it started, I couldn't stop my thinking from splintering off into question after question. For instance, Fin was in the convenience store down the street from the post office. I know that Miss Zelda was a member of God's Own. God's Own knew exactly who Fin was. Fin probably knew Miss Zelda was a member of God's Own. How had those two existed in their charades for so long without outing each other? It didn't make any sense.

"It's OK, Hez. You had no way of knowing."

Fin clasped my shoulder as he spoke. It jostled me back to reality.

"But we have him now, so we need to move on to the next part of our plan. Surely, they are aware he's gone, and they can guess we'll be here for Greg next. We have to get to him before they have a chance to kill him first."

We already knew the rooms inside were too small to bring Vrail in, so we relied on some of my smaller, or more size appropriate friends, to help inside. They were all in place already, except for one. He was waiting until Vrail sent us all inside. We all placed a hand on her and she sent us – Fin, Thread, Dust, Puff, Lincoln, and me – into a small living room that was downstairs. As we appeared in the room, the snake appeared in the hall next to us. She was there to keep guard at the stairs that we would take up to the room Greg was in.

Single file, we all ran up the stairs, Fin carrying Lincoln. Puff reached the top of the stairs first. He released a growl that was mightier than his size and a ball of lighting shot through the length of the hallway. When the rest of us reached the top, we saw bodies splayed on the floor from one end of the hall to the other. I don't think he killed them, but they were definitely going to be unconscious for some time.

I had another friend waiting for us up there. The hall was small, and we were all crammed in it, trying not to step on bodies. From under an end table, a bright-blue lizard with eight legs crawled out and scurried to the closed door. In a flash, he shot out his tongue, which grew to the size of a baseball bat as it hit the center of the door. The door exploded at the blow and flew apart into splinters. I released the lizard and we all rushed inside the small room.

Greg was on the bed, drugged. Not to the point he was unconscious, but he was not able to react quickly, and probably had slowed thinking. There were three other people in the room. Two I didn't recognize, and the overseer. The two strangers stood on either side of the bed, while the overseer sat in a small wingback chair in the corner farthest from the door.

The second the overseer was in sight, Thread started to pull strings, but before she could go through anyone, the woman to the left of the bed raised a hand and everyone was frozen in place. Everyone except me. Later, Thread told me it felt like a spike going through her brain that prevented her from accessing her abilities. The man to the right of the bed reached his arm toward Greg. A glowing blade extended from his hand to Greg's throat. It looked like it was made of light, like a larger version of what Miss Zelda held to my throat when I was nailed to the stake.

The overseer opened his mouth to speak, but before he could, the vent grate toward the ceiling burst off the wall and Boon flew out, flying toward the head of the woman who was keeping the others at bay. Keeping one arm outstretched at us, she swung up the other arm knocking him to the ground before his tiny hammer could hit her head. He slammed into the wall and fell to the ground.

The second the woman hit Boon, Puff growled and bellowed and charged for a blow. The man with the blade of light raised his other hand and the ball of lighting meant for the woman blew back and sent Puff flying out of the room. That was it, that was the point I couldn't see past when I pushed forward. None of us knew what was going to happen from there.

Now it's already happened and I'm trying to think back on the details. Before writing this down, I asked the others to clarify some details from their perspective. I was farthest into the room and they all blocked my view of the door, so I couldn't see everything. They couldn't add much of anything. They said that when they try to remember, it feels like the spike is in their brain again. We've pieced things together as best we can.

As Puff flew out of the room, Boon rose from the ground.

He saw what the man did to Puff, how he hurt him, and he was angry. He did something none of us knew he could do. All it took was a blink and he grew to at least nine feet tall, so tall he had to hunch over in the room. Before he was even full size, he bellowed in a way that hurt everyone in the room, including me. The only two unfazed were Lincoln and the overseer. The woman lost her hold on the others and the man's sword of light shattered. There was still nothing any of us could do. The scream from Boon was as debilitating as whatever the woman had been doing.

Boon's hammer had grown along with him. He swung it in a wide arc and it smashed right through the woman's head and into the wall. It was a quick death. Not so for the man. Boon reached over the bed, and with one hand grabbed the man by the throat and pulled him over. Boon pinned him against the wall, feet off the ground, and held him there, slowly choking. Before he died, Boon bit into the man's face and ripped huge chunks of his skin off, then spat them to the ground. Boon made him suffer for hurting Puff.

After the man was dead, Boon let him drop to the ground and reduced in size as he ran out of the room to Puff. As soon as I was able, I ran out too. Fin, Lincoln, Thread, and Dust were left in the room with Greg and the Overseer. Puff was not moving when I got to the hall, but he didn't appear to be injured either, not visibly. Boon was at his side, stroking his head. Puff's eyes opened and he gave a little snuff as he got back up on his feet. He looked dazed but seemed like he'd be OK.

I left him there with Boon and walked back into the room. Fin sat on the bed next to Greg to check his pulse, his pupils, and for any signs of injury. Thread had an arm raised and a small incision was showing in the cheek of the overseer. Dust eyed him as one of his hands was turning the color of sand and started to flake off, slowly. The twins were both prepared to make his last moments as painful as they could.

"Stop," Fin said. He was off the bed and looking at them both.

They didn't protest or question him. They did exactly what he said and stopped.

"He deserves it, we all know he deserves it. But we need to hand him over to the others. They can lock him away, use him for intel. He'll have more information in him than any of the grunts we've managed to hold in the past."

Fin walked around the bed, drew out one of the sticks on his back, and swung it against the side of the overseer's head, knocking him unconscious. We could have asked Boon to do it, but after what we'd just seen, Boon would likely have killed him. Fin and I carried the overseer outside while Thread and Dust got Greg off the bed and each gave him a shoulder to lean on while they walked out. I hadn't noticed before, but Lincoln had gone out to the hall and was hugging Puff as he sat there on his back legs. The three of them, Lincoln, Puff, and Boon, all got up as we came out in the hall. We were quite the procession, going down the stairs. Once we were on the lower level, we saw there were bodies and pieces of bodies everywhere. The guards had stayed in the basement, ready to be called. When they were, they were met by a giant snake just waiting to rip them to pieces. It looked like she had squeezed a few so hard they popped. At the bottom of the steps, I thanked the snake and released her back to her realm. I'd finally realized she was a she. Not from anything as definite as a physical trait, just a feeling. Like I'd gotten from Vrail after spending enough time with her.

Vrail was in the yard, worked up into a stressed-out state. She dropped her head and nuzzled me, then quickly made her way to Puff. She pushed Lincoln and Boon away and licked him. He squirmed and tried to get away from her. She held him down with a paw and kept licking him. I considered calling The Healer, but Puff really didn't seem to need it.

Fin and I looked up in the air above the house.

"Guess we won't need him. You should let him go now."

As Fin spoke, the others looked up in the air to where Big Green hovered. I released him and sent him back to his spacelike realm. He was our last option, and on a timer. We knew about how long it was going to be to the point I couldn't see past, and we gave it another ten minutes after that. If by then we all weren't outside, Big Green would start bombing around the house. He wasn't supposed to destroy the house, it was just meant to be a distraction if we needed it.

I looked around at everyone. I used to be so alone, but now, here was this group of family, friends, and special friends.

"We're going to need a bigger cabin."

PART THREE

One

Oh my gosh, so much shuffling over the past few months. It's kept me from writing as often as I was.

We took the overseer to The Group. On occasion I call them Myrtle's Minions, really just to get a chuckle out of Thread and Dust. They're holding him and trying to get info from him. It doesn't sound like they've been successful yet, though I'm sure they would be if they gave Thread and Dust a few minutes with him. Losing a few limbs might loosen his tongue. Or they could let me call the snake for assistance. For some reason Myrtle seemed hesitant for any of my friends to be in her compound.

We all decided we wanted to stay together, but away from the compound. Vrail, Fin, and I went on a search for a new cabin. We needed it to be bigger than my previous one, but just as secluded. It needed the same constraints as before, being abandoned and such. It took a few days to find something suitable. During that time, Greg was in my bed upstairs, so he had his own room to recuperate from the drugs they had him on. Fin slept on the couch. Lincoln insisted on sleeping on the floor with Vrail, Puff, and Boon. Thread and Dust had their tent outside, and I got one for me to put up near theirs. The three of us stayed up late most nights, roasting marshmallows, exploring the woods, and I would spend time bringing my friends over from the other realms for Thread and Dust to meet. Fin spent his waking time sitting in the bedroom, monitoring Greg.

The lack of utilities at the cabin made things awkward while we were all staying there.

Eventually, we found the perfect place. We haven't figured out exactly where it is yet. We don't even know what country it's in. Unless you ask Vrail to take you somewhere specific, you don't really know where you're going. This place has enough space for all of us to have our own room. Even so, Thread and Dust picked one room together. Fin and I chose rooms across from each other. Greg is down the hall from us, and we put a smaller bed in his room for Lincoln. Most nights I hear Greg sneak out of his room and go to Fin's. Fin still hasn't told me, but I think there was more meaning to it when he told me he and Greg were partners. I don't want him to think he needs to hide anything from me, and I'm happy for him to be happy, but I don't want to press him to talk about something he may not be ready to share.

The downstairs is one giant open space, like my old place but blown up on a huge scale. We cushioned part of the floor for Vrail, Puff, and Boon. Boon, by the way, has taken to sometimes remaining small and sometimes going full-size. At first it was disconcerting to walk into the family room and find a nine foot Yeti sitting on the couch and looking out the giant bay windows as if he's contemplating the meaning of life, but now it's old hat. We've lined the walls of the family room with shelves and books. We've all made a few group trips to bookstores to fill out the shelves more fully, but most of the time it's just Fin and me. We try to get as much time to hangout as possible. And of course, there's a giant fireplace that Vrail loves on the days it's cold enough to light it.

This place has water and electricity too. The electricity is from a generator, but getting gas to run it hasn't been an issue. Greg takes care of that. In front of the cabin is all woods. In the back is a lush yard next to a giant lake, backdropped by mountains. There are several patio sets spaced out in the back. Everything is beautiful and peaceful.

I know things won't stay this peaceful for long, so I'm enjoying it while I can.

Two

I'm usually the first one up in the mornings. I get my shower then make coffee and sit out back at one of the patio sets that overlook the water while I wait for others to get up. I had a little surprise this morning, when Greg came outside just seconds after I sat down. We've all been here for months, but Greg and I haven't really spoken all that much, and we haven't been alone together at all. I had the impression that he gets tense around me. I suspected he knows that I know about him and Fin, and he doesn't know how to act around me. He sat down at the little round table with me and placed his cup of coffee next to mine.

"Beautiful morning," he said, staring out over the water. "You and Fin sure did pick the perfect place."

"Thanks, but it was really Vrail. She's amazing. I just give her some basic ideas of what we want, and she takes us places that match up. I wish I knew how she did it."

I've spent a lot of time pondering how Vrail knew where to take me.

"Wish my power worked like that. I have to know specifically where I want to go. I can't work off vague ideas, I really need to see the place first. I don't need to know geographic coordinates or anything, but I have to have seen the place before to get to it. As you showed in the trailer, you obviously know I have to touch something too, to open a void."

Crap, I kind of forgot I had a giant snake subdue and then bite him.

"Um, yeah, sorry about that. I had no idea who you were, other than some member of God's Own. Did it hurt? When she bit you, did it hurt?"

This was becoming an awkward conversation.

"Nah, it was fine. It didn't hurt. It was more like a relief, sort of. Like, I couldn't talk to anyone about what was going on. I couldn't contact Fin or Myrtle. If I did, Lincoln would die. But when that snake bit me, all the stress, anxiety, and fear just went away. I was free to talk as openly as I wanted to. It's hard to explain. It didn't feel like I was compelled to tell the truth, but at the same time I wanted to tell you the truth because I was free to. Boon though, that little guy has a mean swing. Left me with a headache for days."

He had been looking at the lake, but then he changed position in his chair and looked directly at me. When I noticed I turned to look at him. He continued.

"It was me, I'm the one who put the needle in you in the convenience store. I had already taken someone else into the back room. They came out behind Fin and drugged him. If Fin hadn't been distracted at the sight of me, there's no way they would have been able to take him. I'm the one who took you both to the congregation."

His voice stayed steady, but he'd gone pale white. It looked like he was going to be sick all over the table. I picked up my coffee just in case.

"Yeah, I figured. After I saw you make that void in the wall of the congregation and go through with the overseer, I figured you were the one who had taken us."

I was glad my rational assumption was correct.

"At the time I didn't know what they were going to do to either of you. I'm not stupid, I knew it wasn't going to be good.

But I had no idea they were going to nail you to a stake and kill Fin in front of you."

His gaze was intense.

"If it wasn't for me, none of that would have happened. I did that to you. I did that to you, and Fin."

"Greg, you're not stupid. And neither are we. They had your nephew. What else were you supposed to do? Right now, if they took Fin, and if there was a very real threat that they could kill him, I just, I don't even know. I don't even know what I would do."

I really don't. Would I do whatever they asked to try and save him? Or would I scorch them all while trying to save Fin? I'm sure that if I told Vrail I wanted to go from congregation to congregation, or compound to compound, she could do it. I could bring Big Green with me, just level everything that organization owns. Then go member by member to their homes, destroy them all. Maybe that's what I should do now. Just end things.

My internal monologue must have gone on a bit too long because Greg's eyebrows were scrunched down as he looked at me.

"I'm sorry. I really am. I just didn't see another way to protect Lincoln. And then the drugs they had me on, I couldn't think for myself, I couldn't tell up from down most of the time. Fin talks about you non-stop, but it doesn't sound like he's told you much of anything about me. Lincoln is my only family. My childhood was nothing to be envied. It was like one bad event kept leading to another. Lincoln is the only family I have now, the only good family."

"I get it, I really do. Lincoln is to you what Fin is to me. But look around. Everyone here is your family now. I know that's sappy, but it's true. This isn't God's Own or Myrtle's group. No one is here because they are being told to be here, no one is working a job, no one is being controlled. Everyone here is here because they want to be. Fin and I are blood, but I would do anything for Thread and Dust. I know you and I don't know each other very well, but I know how close you and Fin are, how much he cares for you. We all do. Because of that, we all put our lives on the line to get you and Lincoln to safety."

I wanted to talk him out of feeling like an outsider. It was a feeling I was remarkably familiar with.

"Fin. He... I wish... there's just this stuff that you don't..."

I knew what he wanted to tell me, but I wondered if Fin had asked him not to.

"You mean about you and Fin being *partners*? You know his room is right across from mine. I hear you going in there nearly every night. I think Thread and Dust know too. The very first time Fin talked about you and referred to you as his partner, I took it to mean you'd go on missions together. When he talked about you then, Thread and Dust got a bit awkward. Fin didn't seem to notice, but I did. At the time it didn't make sense, but it does now. If Fin doesn't want to talk to me about it, it's fine. I don't want to push him on something so personal. If he does want to talk, I'll be here."

I wanted Greg to know that I wasn't an asshole. Maybe he thought that after being in God's Own for so long that their homophobic teachings rubbed off on me.

Greg's jaw had dropped a bit while I was talking, but when I finished his mouth had formed a smile. He looked relieved.

I went on. "Beside, we should all be thanking you. When God's Own had Lincoln, you could have told them where Myrtle's compound was. You could have told them about Fin's ability. The information you had, you could have compromised a lot of people, but you didn't."

His face flushed. He looked embarrassed.

"They asked a lot about Fin, but nothing related to his power. They wanted to know where the compound was, but I told them that the group moves around a lot to avoid being found. I took them to an old bunker that was used years and years ago and told them that was where the group was last."

"Fin, Thread, and Dust, they all call what we can do *abilities*, but you call them *powers*. Why?"

It was just a semantic thing, but I got the feeling there was something to it.

"Man, you are opening a can of worms with this." He chuckled and looked up to the sky." OK, I feel that an ability is basically something that most people can do. You just happen to be better at it, but within normal limits. Say, like, running for instance. Most people can run, but some people are much, much faster than others. Those who are faster have this ability to go faster that others don't. What we can do, these aren't things others can do. We have power. Some of us at a vastly different level than others. What I wouldn't give for yours. You may not be able to harness the powers yourself, but you can access all the beings who really own the powers the rest of us just borrow. You are limitless. If I had that, I swear, I would end God's Own. Fin and the others, they don't like me calling what we have power. I won't do their arguments justice, so you should ask them about it sometime."

His eyes looked over the lake again. I think he was still thinking about what he would do to God's Own if he was in my place.

I still had a few things on my mind that I'd wanted to ask Greg but hadn't had the opportunity to before.

"Is it OK if I ask you a few questions? About your time with God's Own?" I sounded hesitant, which is how I felt.

"I thought you might want to. Go ahead." As he said that, Fin came out with a cup of coffee and joined us. He clapped us both on our backs and sat down between us. I decided to continue. Fin had likely asked the same questions already.

"At the congregation, that night we were all there, there were dozens and dozens of members of God's Own, but you, Miss Zelda, and the guy who killed Fin are the only ones who used abilities. Then, when we went to get Lincoln, it was only normal people guarding him. After that we went to get you, and there were those two others in the room, the woman and the man. They definitely had abilities. They could have killed or taken all of us if Boon hadn't been there. How many people with abilities do they have?"

"I can't say precisely. They kept me drugged the entire time. I didn't see many people other than the two they had in my room and the overseer. When he needed me to use my power, or go do something, he would come personally to give me my orders. Just remember though, God's Own isn't just this local congregation. They exist worldwide. Myrtle's group has accumulated a ton of information on them. A lot of that was provided to them by your dad and me. I could get us close to the compounds and your dad could get us inside. Also, your dad, well, if you've never seen him fight, I can tell you no one can stop him once he gets going. We would pull all the documentation we could and give it to Myrtle's think tank to analyze it. From what we've discovered so far, they are primarily normal people. If you have a power, you aren't actually a member—you're a tool. Some are tools willingly because they fall for the messaging, others are forced against their will, like I was, and like they tried to do to you.

Regarding the two in the room with me, I don't know whether they were there willingly or if they were forced in some way to be there."

I suddenly felt bad for those two. If they had been forced to be there, in the same way Greg had been, then maybe they had family members that God's Own had now killed since they would no longer be of use.

"Just one other question for now. The overseer told me, and you told me, that they want me to raise their God. Did you hear or see anything that might indicate, specifically, what it is they want me to do?"

Greg started to speak but hesitated and looked at Fin first.

"We do need to talk about that, but let's get everyone together first. And we want to grab Myrtle too. We may not be directly in her group right now, but she should know this."

Fin placed his hand on mine with a gentle squeeze while he spoke. It told me Greg did know something, and I doubted I was going to like it.

Three

Greg and Fin went to get Myrtle while Thread, Dust, and I stayed behind to make some appetizers, coffee, and tea. Everyone in the cabin, apart from Lincoln, drank coffee, but evidently Myrtle is a tea drinker and won't touch coffee. After about an hour, we were all gathered in the family room, waiting for Fin and Greg to begin. Lincoln played outside with Puff and Boon. Vrail sat next to my chair and kept an eye on Myrtle, who sat on the couch with Thread and Dust. Greg and Fin shared the love seat.

"Myrtle, is there any info from the overseer yet?" Fin started with this question.

"No, he hasn't spoken one word. You would all know that already if you would come back. It doesn't make any sense to split our efforts like this. We can accomplish more together than we can apart. With Hezekiah and Greg, we could go anywhere, track down all the information we need to stop God's Own from manipulating any more of our kind."

As she did in the conference room in her compound, she sounded kind and compassionate.

"What we do know is that God's Own is centralizing more and more of those in their ranks who have abilities. They have seen a bit of what all of you, particularly Hezekiah, can do. They are massing for either protection, or a fight."

Fin looked at Greg and continued without addressing her comments about splitting our groups.

"We suspected as much. We've known since that night in the

congregation that they want Fin to raise who they believe is their God, but we knew nothing about who that God is, what it can do, or what exactly they wanted Hez to do. While they had Greg, he heard bits of information here and there. Not everything, but enough for us to start putting some pieces together. Greg?"

"Yeah, like Fin said, I didn't hear anything completely. And what I did hear sounds ludicrous. However, taking what I heard along with information we've already gained, things get a littler clearer. God's Own was formed two centuries ago. Their founder was human, but he had witnessed others with power and decided they were tools to be used. One of the first people they took control of had power like Hez's. Not the same, just similar. She could project herself to the other realms, but she couldn't call any of the beings back. She couldn't access their powers in any way. She couldn't project out into our normal world, or to the future. All this extra stuff that Hez can do, she couldn't. They tested her power and found that she could bring others with her to the other realms. It took skin contact. If she was touching someone else while she projected, they would project with her."

I don't know what information he had heard and what information was already known. It was all new to me.

I looked over at the couch and saw that Myrtle held her teacup in one hand and twiddled the fingers of her other hand. The tea raised above and out of the cup and shaped like a twirling ballerina. Myrtle saw my surprised look and the tea dropped back into her cup.

"Sorry dear, I'm hydrokinetic. It's like being telekinetic but it only works on liquid. If the liquid turns to ice or steam, I'm afraid I'm completely useless. Go on Greg."

"Something they didn't realize at first was that when she took someone else with her, once they returned to our world, that person had limited access to the power of the being in the realm they had gone to. They did more and more extensive tests and found that there was a correlation to how long they spent in the realm, and how long the individual retained the power. This is where things get spotty, and I'm not sure if they knew what was possible, or if they were hypothesizing and hoping for the best.

"They decided that their founder would go with her to a different realm. Once there, the founder killed the girl's body. If she came back, then so would their founder. They figured that if she were dead, but his body remained living, he would stay in the other realm until he was brought back. They also figured that once the girl was out of the picture, their founder might be able to figure out how to move himself between the realms. Their plan relied on someone else in the future being able to visit the realms and pull him back. They've kept his body alive for 200 years. I don't know how, but they have. They want Hez to find him and bring him back to his body. After 200 years of absorbing powers, he could be devastating to the world.

"So, it isn't a prophecy or anything mystical like that. They didn't specifically foresee Hez and his abilities although I'm sure they would love everyone to believe they had that level of foresight. What they've done to Hez, they've done to many others. They have someone in their group who can feel the level of power someone will have. If someone has a high enough level, God's Own does what they can to control and shape them. They've just been waiting for someone with the right type of power to come along to complete their plan. If they can't get Hez to help them, their plan is to kill him. They fear that Hez might track down their founder in the other realms and kill him there. He doesn't get access to the powers until he returns to his body, so he'll be helpless there. In their eyes, either Hez must help them, or die so he can't kill their founder, who they now believe is a god."

Everyone's eyes went from Greg to me. I looked at Greg.

"What happened to the girl? When they killed her body, I mean. Did she remain in the other realm too, or did she really, fully die?"

"I don't know, and I don't think they do either."

I looked over at Fin.

"Do you think that I can take others to the realms too? I've never tried, I never even thought of that as a possibility."

"I'm not sure, there's so much that's unique about you. I don't think anyone knows what all you're capable of. Or if you have any limitations."

He looked like a genuinely concerned father.

"Well, we should test it sometime. If I need to face him there, it might be helpful to have someone else there too."

Me, a teenager, needing to fight a 200-year-old man in a different realm. My life has become outrageous.

"We volunteer, we'll do it!" Thread shouted out as she and Dust raised their hands in the air.

Myrtle placed a hand on Thread's knee.

"Girls, perhaps that's an experience he'd like to share with his father first."

"No way," Thread argued." What if it doesn't work? What if Hez can get someone there but can't bring them back. Fin is too important. We can't take that chance with him."

"I'm no more important than anyone else here. Every one of you have active powers that will be useful if this comes down to a fight in our world. What am I going to do? Have every enemy kill me one by one on a battlefield?"

His eyes hadn't left mine.

"And if they have someone else who can take away, or limit our abilities like that woman did? You're the best hand-to-hand fighter here, and you're the best tactician we have."

Thread wouldn't let it drop.

"I'll do it," Greg said. "If there is an issue and Hez can get me there but can't get me back, maybe my power will let me open a void back here. Of all of us, I stand the best chance. Even if he can get me back here, it would be a good test for my own powers too, to see if I can open a void from another realm back here. If a fight of the magnitude we assume is coming, we should all be pushing the limits of our powers."

All eyes went from me to Greg. He was right.

"I don't know. I get it, what you're saying makes sense. But we just got you back. I can't… we can't lose you again."

I could hear the emotion in Fin's voice.

"I think this isn't really an issue. We're talking about a risk that we don't even know exits. I mean, it doesn't make much sense to think I could take someone with me but not bring them back. I get it, it's a possibility, but a really, really remote one based on how my abilities have worked so far. If I was hung up on the risks of using my abilities, I never would have gone out to the field to test them in the first place. Besides, I have another option in mind. Why not try taking two instead of one?"

I got up and walked over to the couch and asked Thread, Dust, and Myrtle to get up. I sat down in the middle. I looked over at Fin and Greg.

"Come over here. Each of you take a hand."

Their eyebrows went up and they gave each other a look before walking over to sit down, flanking me. They each took a hand, locking our fingers together. I released Vrail back to her cracked earth place. I tried to really feel Fin and Greg, not just physically, but feel them on a different level. Then I pushed.

All three of us appeared in the cracked earth place. Vrail was walking around and stretching. When I'm in the realms or when I push out or forward, my projected form is in the clothes and accessories I've mentioned before. Fin and Greg both appeared in their tactical gear. Vrail took off at a full run, doing laps and zigzagging. She was so fast. At first, I thought something was wrong, but then I remembered it had been such a long time since she'd been back there, she was probably just happy and blowing off some steam.

Fin and Greg released my hands and we stood there.

"This is Vrail's home?" Fin asked.

"Yeah, I have no idea if others are here or not. It seems like there is one being for each realm, but I don't know if they are just a sort of representative, or if they are the only one."

"It's beautiful. I couldn't have imagined it like this, even after hearing you describe some of these places," Greg said. He looked over at Fin and they both smiled.

Fin grabbed me into a hug. "You will just never stop amazing me."

"Want to go somewhere really trippy?" I asked. I wanted to see if I could shuffle them along with me between realms before we tried going back.

They each grabbed a hand and I thought about where I wanted to take us. Everything around us moved. Suddenly we were floating in space, Big Green right in front of us.

"What the fu—" Greg started, but Fin cut him off.

"Hey! Don't cuss in front of Hez!" Fin was just being a dad.

"We're in space, how are we breathing?" Greg asked.

I answered, "I don't think it's really space. It's just another realm that looks like space."

From there I took us to the dead forest where the Glowing Woman stayed. Once we were there Greg touched the ground to open a void back to the cabin. It opened, and after a brief conversation between him and Fin, Greg walked through it and the void closed.

It was obvious that Fin was nervous about whether it had worked or not, so even though I wanted to show him more realms, when he took my hand, I took us back to our bodies.

The three of us still sat on the couch, fingers locked together. We were all there and in our bodies.

"You made it back!" Fin said as he looked over at Greg.

"Uh, yeah, but not the way I expected." He sounded fine, but a little weirded out.

"Yeah, you can say that," Thread agreed." No void appeared on this end. You were all just slumped over, then suddenly Greg's head lifted, he was back here, but you two weren't."

"It seems like I can open a void from those realms, but it takes me back into my body, not to a place."

That was an interesting development. I figured that the void would bring the projected version of Greg back and then he'd just settle back into his body.

Fin and Greg recounted what they'd seen and what it felt like. After seeing Vrail run around her realm like she did, I released Puff and Boon as well. I loved having them all around, but I need to be more mindful about the impact it might have on them, being away from their own homes for so long. By then, Lincoln was back inside, sitting on the floor with Thread and Dust.

After talking for a few minutes, Myrtle asked Greg to take her back home. Greg opened a void and they walked through, but before stepping through Greg said he'd be gone for a bit because he wanted to grab some more of his things.

Fin put an arm on my shoulders and said, "Let's go for a walk. There's some stuff I'd like to talk about."

Four

We walked down to the lake and meandered along the rocky shore.

"When I met your mom, we fell in love hard and fast. It was one of the best times of my life. She had always had days where she was just a bit off. Her mood would be flat, or she'd stay in bed half the day and act like it was completely normal when she'd get up. Other days she seemed to have limitless energy and constantly be on the run for one thing or another. I hadn't worried too much about it. I didn't think things would get so bad in her head that she'd leave, but she did. After she left, after she took you and your brothers, I was all alone for such a long time. My focus was always to find you, no matter what it took. Back then I didn't know anything about God's Own or what they were doing to her.

I told you that I got that job at the newspaper and that's when I started getting my life together. It was then that I first got introduced to Myrtle's group. Greg was that introduction. He'd been working at the paper as a reporter. One day, he came down to the printing level and introduced himself. He said he was interested in all the operations of the paper because he wanted to run one of his own one day. We hit it off immediately. Anyway, after a few weeks, one thing led to another and he told me about his ability. He told me he knew about mine as well. He said he was part of a group that helped find and protect others like us. He introduced me to Myrtle and everything snowballed from there.

I know you don't know her much yet, but she really is a fantastic person. The decisions she makes, the recommendations she gives, they are because she wants to keep everyone safe. She'll take risks if they are absolutely necessary, but her concern is always with the safety of people like us. I stayed with them but continued to work at the paper. Greg would move us between the compound and work each day. We started spending more and more time together. While I was put through training, Myrtle found our abilities and skills were compatible. She sent us out on missions together. We just clicked. We had successful mission after successful mission.

I think I'm turning this into a longer story than it needs to be, because I'm terrified to tell you something that I want to tell you. I don't want to have secrets from you, and I'm not ashamed of this, but I know how much time you spent with God's Own. I know you know how to think for yourself, but still, you're young, and impressions can be difficult to shake."

He was hem hawing.

"Whatever it is, you can just tell me. There is pretty much nothing you could say that's going to make me think badly of you. I've wanted a dad my entire life. Now I have you, and you're even more amazing than I had ever hoped for."

I was sincere in every word.

"I love him, Hez. Greg. I love him. He isn't just a friend, or a partner to go on missions. We are together, and we have been for a long time. We haven't told anyone about it. Not because we are ashamed, but just because you never know how people will react to a relationship like ours."

He was looking at the ground. I knew he wasn't ashamed of himself, but he was worried about how I would take his news.

It was my turn to hug him.

"I love you so much, thank you for sharing this with me. Don't hide it, not from anyone. I know you loved Mom once, but I didn't have any delusions about you two getting back together and us being a big happy family. Those hopes sailed a long time ago. As for you and Greg being together, he's a great guy, really hot too. Does he know he looks like a comic book hero? You're both lucky. Be who you are and trust your friends. Besides, if anyone objects, I'll kick them out of the cabin. Or better yet, Vrail can eat them."

I knew it wouldn't come to that. I knew Thread and Dust understood what was going on, and I was sure they were just as happy for him as I was.

"I don't understand how you turned out so normal and rational after everything you've been through. It would be so easy for you to hate everything and everyone, and no one would be able to blame you."

"Well, I wouldn't go that far. I did kill my brother, and dozens of guys when we were rescuing Lincoln and Greg. Oh yeah, and all those people on the stage of the congregation after they staked me and killed you. I didn't even hesitate in any of those instances. I also don't regret any of it. I do hate, but it's directed at God's Own, not anyone else. So, I think all that takes me out of the *normal* category. I'll give you rational though, I do think I've stayed rational, given everything that's happened."

I was matter of fact about it all.

"Hal would have killed you eventually. I read your journal, remember? That was clearly where it was headed. You did what you had to do to survive. And all those guys at the houses where Lincoln and Greg were held, you did that for me. I can't thank you enough for that. Without you, I wouldn't have Greg back."

Five

When we were back inside Fin shared with Thread and Dust what he had shared with me. They said it was about time and that they figured it out a long time ago. Lincoln had already known. It sounds like Greg told him the first night we came to this cabin. Fin looked relieved and relaxed in a way he hadn't been before. Apart from Greg, we must be the three most important people in his life, so of course he was going to be anxious to share that part of himself with us, not knowing how we would react to it. I had called Vrail back. She's my best friend and I wanted her there to hear what Fin was telling us.

As the discussion wrapped up, a void opened and Greg came through.

"The overseer is gone!"

He was out of breath.

"Hez's mom and brothers helped him escape, they all left the compound. Myrtle is still trying to figure out how it could have happened. It was while she was here with us. She's trying to get all the surveillance videos, but it looks like some of the cameras were shut off or unplugged or something. They're evacuating now. If the overseer knows how to get back to the compound, they're all in danger!"

My eyes were dead. Fin saw that as he looked at me. I reached up, blank expression on my face, and put a hand on Vrail. Fin knew what I was going to do. With one hand he grabbed my arm, and with the other he grabbed the person standing nearest him, Dust.

I told Vrail to take me to wherever my mom was. We appeared in the middle of a street, a maroon car heading straight for us. We could all see my mom driving. She wasn't slowing down. Dust lifted an arm. I jumped at her to stop her from dusting my mom, but Fin held me back.

"It's OK. She's just going to stop the car; she isn't going to hurt anyone."

The car slowed, then came to a stop ten feet or so from us. I was confused. I knew Thread mentioned that she and Dust had secondary powers, but I wasn't sure exactly what Dust had just done. Fin explained before I could ask.

"Dust can slow things, Thread can speed them up. It doesn't have anything to do with slowing or speeding time, they can just control how quickly objects, or people, can move."

The driver's door flew open and Mom came barreling out.

"Sinners! You're all sinners! You will all burn in hell!"

It was unreal. She was back to the fire and brimstone version of herself. But the woman who had been controlling her was dead, it couldn't be happening again. Initially she was unfocused and her gaze moved all around. Then she focused on me.

"You, you're the worst of them! I always knew you were from Satan. You need to come with me right now. Get in this car! God's Own will find some use for you, you pathetic little bastard!"

My jaw dropped. I couldn't believe what she was saying. I'd pulled out the other woman. The Dark Woman version of Mom went back in her body. I saw it. She was normal again. When she was there with me and Fin. It was her. How could it all have started again? I grabbed Fin by the arm and told him to get ready to catch me. I momentarily pushed out, but at our location. When the other woman was in Mom, I was able to see her. This time, I didn't see anything. It was just Mom. There was no one else inside her. I went back to my body.

"There isn't anyone else there. It's just her. Fin, what's going on? What's happened to her?"

My voice was monotone again.

"I don't know. The last time I saw her she was fine. She was trying to acclimate to everything that had happened, but she was fine."

He spoke slowly, trying to form an idea of what might have gone wrong.

"And you!" She looked right at Fin." I know what you are! You filthy little man! You know what happens to people like you!"

She was bright red with anger, spittle flying from her mouth.

"What do we do? Do we take them back to Myrtle? I don't know what to do." I needed someone else to come up with a plan.

Dust looked like she wanted to kill Mom after hearing how she spoke to me and Fin. She restrained herself.

Fin said, "No, no I don't think we should take her to Myrtle. Not until we know what's going on. We can't take her to the cabin either. It would compromise everyone there. If she isn't being controlled by someone, I don't know what we can do that won't make things worse. I think we have to let them go."

I didn't want to accept that, but I didn't know what else to do. I couldn't have her around me and the others when she was like this. I'd worked too hard to get past all of that abuse. I couldn't bring it into my new home, with my new family. I also didn't think taking her to Myrtle was a good idea. She had already been there, and whatever had gone wrong, it happened there.

I looked up at Fin.

"Yeah, OK, but we need to find out what happened, and find out quickly."

I considered asking if we should see if my brothers wanted to come with us, but I looked in the car and their expressions gave their answer without my asking it. Their arms were crossed and their eyes were daggers.

"The overseer," Fin was almost muttering. "He isn't with them. We need to get back to the cabin, we need to get back to everyone and figure this out."

"Should I ask Vrail to take us to him? Try to capture him quickly?"

As Fin answered, Mom continued to rant in the background.

"No, not until we know what's going on. If this was planned, he may have others with abilities with him. It's too dangerous without having more information."

The three of us put our hands on Vrail. As we left, we could still hear Mom's screams about sins, filth, and the fire of hell.

Six

Back at the cabin Fin was slumped in the chair I normally sat in. Vrail sat next to him and looked worried about him. I paced around the room and filled everyone in on what had happened, what Mom had said. Greg had gone back to the compound to help evacuate people. I considered going with Vrail to help, but Fin looked shellshocked. I wouldn't leave him like that.

"She was so vicious. I know, you've talked about what she was like, and I read it in your journal. But I've never seen her that way in person. That was horrible. Was that really what your life was like all that time you were with her?" He looked at the floor in front of the chair.

"Pretty much, yeah, most of the time. Until she just stopped getting out of bed completely. That was about the time things started to turn around, for a while at least. It's all really been ups and downs. I guess we're dropping into another down now."

He's read everything I'd written, so I couldn't really sugarcoat anything.

"And then your brothers, on top of that?" He was still keeping his eyes on the floor.

"Well, that was really Hal. Grady and Jeremiah were always along for the ride and ready to jump on the anti-Hez bandwagon whenever they could, but if Mom or Hal wasn't around to prod things, they kind of acted like I didn't exist, which was great for me. Sometimes, I have the feeling that Jeremiah might not be so bad, but I really don't know. You saw them both in the car, obviously they sided with Mom again."

I was relieved by that. It wasn't exactly intentional, but since I pulled that other woman out of Mom's body, I hadn't visited them at all. Not Mom, or my brothers. I didn't send them any type of message through the others. I just completely cut them out. There were so many memories tied to them all, it has been easier for me not being around them. Just seeing them, it sends these negative thoughts coursing through me. I didn't want to see them, and I definitely didn't want to bring them to the cabin, even if they had wanted to come. I was so happy with my new life, my dad, my friends. I didn't want any shadows of my past hanging around.

"Everyday I should say I'm sorry, Hez. I should have done more. I should have stood up to Myrtle earlier, tried to get you away from them earlier."

He looked at me then, fighting tears. My heart ached, and I also realized in that moment how much I loved that he wasn't afraid to show his emotions so openly. I should try to be more like him. That was also when I learned Myrtle was the reason I was left to suffer in that trailer. She was preventing Fin from helping me. Why would she do that?

"It's all done, and now we're here together. All of us." I waved an arm at Thread, Dust, and Vrail." I have the family I always wanted, and the past can't jump up and take me back. I know how hard it is to see her that way, but we can't dwell on it either. We need to find out what's making her behave this way now. Then we can plan a way to help her."

I tried my best to sound calm and brave. In fact, I was terrified that something could happen, and I would end up in the grip of Mom or God's Own again. That we wouldn't be able to stop it from happening. But that fear wasn't what anyone needed to hear.

"I told you he's the toughest person in the room." Thread looked from Fin to me.

"Yes, Thread, you're right. Tougher than me for sure. Look at me, a few insults from her and I'm ready to bawl and crawl under the covers. Meanwhile, you dealt with that for what must have felt like a lifetime, and you just want to help her."

He smiled, but I could still see tears in his eyes ready to drop.

A void opened and Greg walked through with a woman I hadn't seen before. She appeared to be in her mid-thirties and was wearing a floral dress similar to the kind Thread and Dust would wear when they weren't in their tactical gear. Her makeup was applied so indelicately it looked like she took a shotgun blast of cheap makeup straight to the face.

"Everyone is out, we got everyone to the next location. Myrtle set the safety timer. In about ten minutes the compound will be an inferno."

Right as Greg finished talking, Fin walked across the room, put a hand behind Greg's head, and kissed him in front of everyone. Seeing that, seeing how obvious their love was for each other, my heart rose.

"Well, so, I guess you told them all. Man, I hope you told them all, and that wasn't how they found out. Tell me you told them all."

Greg's grin was huge as he spoke.

"Just before you came to tell us what had happened, so yes, they knew already." Quickly, the grin on Fin's face disappeared. "Dammit, I didn't think, my journals, and the chest in my room! We have to go get them!"

Chest? I'd forgotten about the chest I saw in his room. It was chained shut. I still don't know what's in that thing.

"It's OK. As everyone else prepared to move, I cleared out your room. It's all safe. It's all in your room upstairs here. If you want to take is somewhere else, we can do that." They held hands as Greg explained what he'd done.

Fin placed a hand on the back of Greg's neck.

"Since when did you move a step ahead of me. I thought that was usually my thing."

"Well," Greg looked over at me, looked around the whole room. "You've had a bit on your mind lately. I think we can call it a fluke, seeing as how this is the first time I've ever thought about something before you."

I hope that one day I have the type of relationship they do.

"Dr Appleton," Thread said, and eyed the woman who came through with Greg. "Why are you here?"

She asked what the rest of us should have asked right away.

"Thread, I hope you and your sister are doing well." Dr Appleton clasped her hands together in front of her. "I have a theory on what happened to Dahlia."

It was weird hearing someone call my mom by her name. Usually people just said, *your mom* or *Hez's mom*. Hearing her called Dahlia felt wrong in some way.

"What's your theory Doctor?" Fin sounded in control and calm again.

"Wait, first off," I cut in. "Who are you and what kind of doctor are you?"

"Hezekiah, we haven't met yet, but I very much look forward to getting to know you. My name is Abigail Appleton. You can call me Abby, most people do. I'm a psychiatrist."

I noticed that Thread and Dust had their hands balled into fists as the doctor spoke.

"Thanks. So, like Fin asked, what's your theory?" We were all looking at her.

The doctor's left eye squinted a little as she looked at me.

"Interesting that you call him Fin instead of Dad. We should talk about that sometime."

Without even thinking about it, my stance widened, my arms crossed over my chest, and my right eyebrow cocked up. She nodded as if she'd been expecting that. I was ready to sass off in some way, but Fin spoke first.

"What Hez chooses to call me isn't your concern and you are not here to evaluate him. You're here to tell us your theory on Hez's mom. You can do that now, or Greg can take you back to the others."

For emphasis, two things happened. First, Greg slapped his hand on a wall and opened a void. Second, Vrail hackled the hair on her haunches and gave an exceptionally low rumble, eyeing the doctor the entire time.

She raised her hands and faced the palms out toward us.

"I didn't mean any harm, I just said it was interesting and eventually I'd love to speak with Hezekiah and see if I can help him work through some of his past trauma, that's it. But about Dahlia. I think that the person who had taken over her body left a boobytrap inside. We did a lot of tests, and not just the kinds on paper. We had limited equipment, but some of the scans showed a small anomaly we couldn't figure out. Also, there were times when we were talking that she would get a strange look, or say something odd. It became clear that at some point she was just placating us. There was more than that though, but I don't think you want to hear every detail. What it comes down to is that I think her body contained a trap. That if she were to return to it, the trap would activate, and cause a merge."

She lowered her hands during her explanation and placed them in her pockets as she paced a small circle.

"What do you mean, 'a merge'?" Thread asked.

"Hezekiah and Fin described her projection as a Dark Woman. That was the essence of Dahlia. Whether you call it a soul, a projection, essence, it doesn't matter. But the body went on and it can contain memories and feelings of its own. Her essence may not believe in God's Own and may not have done those horrible things to Hezekiah, but her body did. What we are seeing now is a rejoining of body and essence, creating an entirely new version of Dahlia. A mix of her essence's personality and experience with her body's personality and experience. And then on top of that, her pre-existing mental illness is exacerbating everything. I think that for a while she might have moments of lucidity where her real essence comes through, but once the merge is complete, there's no predicting what her personality is going to be."

She stopped moving and looked up at us all. She was smiling. None of us were.

"Can you stop it, reverse it?" Greg asked, still holding Fin's hand.

"No, I can't. I don't even understand how it's happening or how the trap worked. I don't know that anyone can stop or reverse it."

Now she had her arms crossed.

"So, beyond a theory, you're saying you're useless in this situation," Thread said flatly. "I think you can leave then."

The doctor looked over at Fin as if she expected his support, but Fin looked at Greg, who opened a void again. The doctor looked around at each of us, rolled her eyes, and walked through the void shaking her head the entire time.

"I don't like her," I said to no one in particular.

Thread reached out and took Dust by the hand. They both looked at me, "Welcome to the club."

Seven

We spent hours brainstorming, trying to figure out what to do next. None of it involved tracking down and recapturing the overseer. It was all about what we could do for my mom. Fin and Greg had done missions across the entire world. They made many connections and knew many people with various abilities. They ran through them as quickly as they could to figure out if any of them would be useful. Thread and Dust went through the same process. It came to nothing. Everyone I knew with abilities was standing in the room, expect for Myrtle. Also, since I wasn't allowed to associate with anyone outside of God's Own for most of my life, I had no connections outside of those in the room.

It was Fin who thought of something.

"Your journal, you wrote about The Healer. That giant, gold frog. He healed you physically, but he was also able to help calm your mind, help you focus. Do you think that if we got your mom, then you pulled The Healer, that he would be able to help her?"

It was the best and most plausible idea so far.

"I don't know. He's helped me, but I haven't asked him to heal someone else. He did heal my body, even fixed my clothes. The calmness came when he forced me to meditate. I don't know if calming me was an ability of his, or if it was just a result of meditating. It's worth a try. Not here though. I can't. I can't associate her, or my brothers, with this place."

Thread put a hand on my shoulder. "Everyone understands. None of us know everything you've been through. None of us know exactly how you feel, but we all understand the need to divide our past from our present and future. If we do this, you pick the place. We will all be there for you."

Though it was Thread who spoke, everyone's faces shared the same sentiment. After everything I'd been through, how lucky I found myself to find these friends, this family. I'm getting sappier the more I'm around them all. And I love it.

We decided to start with a similar intel collecting approach we had used when planning to rescue Greg and Lincoln. I would push out to find where Mom and my brothers were. Then I'd push forward to give us some forewarning of what to expect. Part went well, part didn't.

I lay down on the couch and pushed out, thinking about my mom. I expected to see her and my brothers in the maroon car she was going to run us down in. Instead, they were in a giant auditorium with thousands of other people. When I say thousands, I mean at least 15,000. It was an indoor assembly arena, similar to a hockey rink. Immediately I knew where they were. God's Own held these annual assemblies of believers. They were held all over the world. They were organized by location. Around six states worth of congregations would assemble twice a year at that arena, to hear special talks and receive new publications. I knew the schedule. There wasn't an assembly planned for this time. This was something different.

There was a small stage with a podium that had been erected in the middle of the floor. To one side was an above ground swimming pool filled with water, ready for baptisms. To the other side of the stage were folding chairs with special congregants in them. If you had done something special or favorable for God's Own, you earned a seat in those chairs, so close to the stage. Sitting in the front row were Mom, Grady, and Jeremiah.

I came back to the cabin and explained the location, setup, and amount of people. Next was for me to push forward, get an idea of what events would be like when we tried to get her, and maybe my brothers.

I dropped back down on the couch but when I tried to push forward a spike shot down the left half of my brain and lodged right behind my eye. I yelped and shot up.

"What's wrong, what happened?" Fin kneeled at my side and ran a hand up and down my back.

"I don't know. I just pushed forward but instead of projecting, it felt like a railroad spike shooting down my head and behind my eye. It was the same way I felt when Boon bellowed in the room when we were getting Greg. That point I couldn't see past."

Until it happened this time, I hadn't really remembered the pain from Boon's scream.

"I remember that," Fin said. "It hurt, badly."

"Us too," Thread added." We couldn't use our abilities. We both tried, but we couldn't get past the pain."

"I was drugged and barely conscious, but the same thing happened to me," Greg said softly.

"Have any of you felt it when you've tried to use your abilities since?" Fin asked the group.

"Well, I was shuffling Myrtle's people around just fine. I didn't feel anything. I haven't tried my other power. We all know it's kind of useless anyway."

I didn't know Greg had a second ability.

"Try it now. Hez, send Vrail back to her realm. Then, look away from Greg, close your eyes, and cover them with your hands."

Weird instructions from Fin, but I trusted him so I did it

without asking questions. Thread and Dust had already taken the steps Fin outlined for me.

As soon as we were all ready, I heard a sound like something whooshing quickly past my ear. Fin patted my back and said, "It's OK, you can open your eyes now."

"It worked just fine, no pain," Greg spoke to all of us.

"What was it? What did you do?" I couldn't stop myself from asking.

"It's stupid. I can make this big flash of light. It doesn't work for illumination like that ball you get from the snake. It's only handy if I need to blind someone temporarily or signal someone from a distance. It's kind of like a flash grenade I guess."

"That sounds really handy," I said. I'd love to be able to blind people if I were in a tough spot. I guess when you have the ability to teleport places, a flashing light probably would seem like a second-rate ability.

"Thread, Dust, I remember you both used your primary abilities on the Overseer after Boon screamed and took down the woman and man in the room with us. Dust used her slowing ability when Vrail took us to Hez's mom. Thread, have you tried your speed ability?"

How does Fin remember that kind of detail? I remember now writing down that Thread was slicing the overseers cheek and Dust was turning his hand to sand after Boon screamed, but that happened months ago. I would never have remembered details that small without prompting.

Thread raised a hand toward a fly that had been buzzing around the room. It was headed for the big bay window. It suddenly moved so quickly that I couldn't see it, but I heard the splat on the window.

"Mine still works," she said as she lowered her hand.

"That's a cool ability," I said, then nodded my head at the window. "But that's gross, Thread."

She smirked, then Greg moved toward the kitchen to grab a paper towel and spray.

"I'll clean it off. I really don't want to look at that all day."

I looked over at Fin." What about you? You have any other abilities to test out?"

He shook his head. "If I have another ability, I haven't discovered it yet."

"So then, everyone is fine and it's just me. But I've gone to the other realms, and I've pushed out and been fine. It's only happening when I try to push forward. Do you think Boon's scream affected me? Or did that woman who blocked your abilities do something to me?"

It was rhetorical. None of us could have an answer for that.

"Should I get Boon? I know he can't talk, but you've all seen how animated he is. Maybe he could pantomime something for us."

Everyone agreed we should start there, so I pushed to the cracked earth place. Once there, I asked Vrail to join us back at the cabin, after giving her a rundown of what I'd discussed with the others. From there I pushed to Boon's location. Once he reluctantly crawled out of his little igloo, I asked him to join us at the cabin.

There we were, all in a circle around tiny Boon, explaining what had happened to me, and explaining that no one else had been affected. I spoke directly to him.

"Boon, is this from your scream?"

His arms were behind his back. He looked at his feet and dug a toe from side to side into the wood floor.

"Boon, is this from your scream?" I asked again. Still

looking down at his feet, his head bobbed slowly up and down.

I felt a wash of relief. I would have felt much more anxiety over it if it had been caused by a member of God's Own.

Fin had a question to ask Boon. "Why? Why did you do that to him? It isn't affecting the rest of us, why Hez?"

I had no idea what kind of answer Boon could mime for that, all he did was look up at Fin and shrug his shoulders.

I took that to mean, *I don't know, maybe I just felt like it.* Everyone else took it to mean, *I don't know, it was an accident.*

"Can you reverse it?" Greg asked.

Boon looked back at his feet. He shook his head from side to side.

"Let's hope it's temporary and will wear off soon, and that it doesn't spread to your other abilities." Fin eyed Boon as he spoke to me.

It sucked, but I couldn't take it out on Boon.

"It's OK Boon, I'm sure it wasn't your intention. We aren't mad at you. Besides, you saved all our lives. If I have to deal with a small limitation and a headache for a bit, it's worth it. Do you want to stay here with us for a while? I can get Puff, too, if you want."

In answer, he ran over to Vrail and placed a hand on her leg as he sat down next to her. I lay back down and brought Puff over. He immediately charged at Boon and they rolled around, wrestling on the floor. Vrail sighed and just let them play.

Eight

We decided to act the same day. We initially thought it might be prudent to wait, see if the assembly would disperse after a few days, but we didn't know how the timing of that might affect the merge that the doctor theorized in my mom. For all we knew, time was of the essence.

"We should tell Myrtle what we're planning," Fin thought out loud.

Greg raised his hand to a wall to open a void, but Fin stopped him.

"No, let's use one of our communicators upstairs." He smiled. "It'll be harder for her to try and talk us out of it than if we were talking in person."

Greg chuckled and they both walked upstairs.

Puff, Boon, and Lincoln were all playing outside again, with Vrail watching over them.

I looked over at Thread. "So, the doctor, what's up with her? Why don't you like her?"

Thread didn't answer immediately. When she did, her voice was slow and measured.

"We've been through a lot, my sister and me. Taken from our parents when we were young, when our abilities first started to show. We were traded around, sold. Various powerful people's playthings. Not powerful with abilities, but still, powerful people. Eventually God's Own heard about us. They came and took us away from that, brought us to America. We thought they were saving us. They weren't. They trained us. They weaponized us. They told us what to do and when to do it. Just as much playthings as we had been before. Then, Fin found us. He'd found some information about us, our background, he made us a priority mission. It wasn't pretty, but he got us out. The more time we spent with him, the more we trusted him. He didn't rescue us to use us. He rescued us to help us.

"Dr Appleton is the only psychiatrist in Myrtle's group. She meets with everyone new. She was fascinated by our past and our abilities. She insisted we meet with her every week, then multiple times a week, then every day. She hounded us, wanted to know every personal, private detail of our lives. She kept wanting us to talk again and again about terrible things we'd been through, and terrible things we'd done. She was making us relive those experiences over and over. That was when Dust stopped speaking to anyone but me.

She wasn't interested in helping us. She just wanted to study us, to keep pushing us to see if we would break, or if it would influence our abilities. We told Fin how we felt and he confronted her. Of course, she tried to dismiss what we'd told him, said we were damaged and dangerous and didn't know what we were talking about. Fin stayed on our side. He ordered an end to our meetings with her. She was furious and went to Myrtle, told her it wasn't safe for us to stay with them unless she was able to continue meeting with us. Myrtle agreed. That's when Greg stepped in. He looked Myrtle right in the eyes and told her she was being manipulated by Dr Appleton, and that if she thought it was in her rights to force Dust and me to do something we didn't want to do, then he, Fin, Dust, and I didn't have any place with them. He opened a void and we were all prepared to walk through. Myrtle reluctantly conceded the issue and said we would not have to do anything we did not want to do. We never met with Dr Appleton again and she's never gotten over it. I think Myrtle still has a grudge against Greg too. That's probably why it was so easy for her to accept that he'd flipped sides and joined God's Own."

The doctor definitely did not sound like someone I wanted to talk to.

"I wasn't sure how much to believe you, when you told me that you and Dust had been in my position before. I do believe you. It must be hard for you to trust others, the same way it is for me."

"At first, yes. It got easier with Fin. He trusted Greg, so our trust extended to him. Fin is a great judge of character. If someone earns his trust, they will have ours. And if they cross him in some way, they will have the two of us to answer to."

I cannot imagine that it would be a pleasant experience for anyone who gets on those two's bad sides. I'm actually surprised the doctor isn't in pieces or a pile of sand.

Fin and Greg came down the stairs and back into the family room. Both looked frazzled.

Thread asked, "What did she have to say?"

Fin and Greg looked at each other, both shaking their heads.

Fin said, "She very explicitly ordered us not to move on the assembly or to get Hez's mom and brothers. She told us that we all had to vacate the cabin and join back up with the group. She said we have no idea what we are doing and we have no right to endanger ourselves by storming an assembly of 15,000 people, and that we are being selfish. She said that the group spent too much time helping and training us for us to throw away our lives on something so fruitless."

"And what did you say?"

There was no way I was going to that group now.

"Before I could respond—" Fin started to say, but he was cut off by Greg.

"I told her to fuck off. Saving one person at a time is what we do, that isn't fruitless or selfish. This is Hez's mom. We help each other. Without that, if we are just members of a group that gives us orders, tells us when and how to use our powers, how are our lives any different than if we were in God's Own?"

He gave my thoughts exactly.

Fin started again. "So we shut off the communicator we were using while she was still screaming orders at us. At this point, that might be a bridge burned."

I didn't care. I don't think anyone in the room did.

Nine

We ran through our plan. A big point was to hurt as few of the people in the bleachers as possible. Most of God's Own were normal people who were very devoted to a Christian-based religion. The majority didn't know that the religion was just a front for a smaller group of people trying to abuse the abilities of those born with them. Most of the members didn't even know about people with abilities. A gathering of the size I saw means that God's Own expects us to come for Mom, and probably the overseer, and they are using regular people as a shield. I didn't really know any of that until the others explained it to me.

That meant that I couldn't really bring in a bunch of the beings from the other realms and just clean house. We needed to be more careful than that. We knew that there would be others with abilities there. Myrtle had told us that God's Own was consolidating their members with abilities in order to oppose us. What we didn't know was where they were. It was possible they had them all located on the flooring, next to the stage. Or, they could have been laced throughout the crowd, which would make it more difficult to keep the normal people safe. Or maybe both of those possibilities. Or neither. Without being able to push forward, I had no idea.

Everyone accepted that Fin had the most knowledge about how God's Own operates and is the best field tactician in our little group. He said it's most likely that the majority of those with abilities would be on the floor, around my mom, brothers, and the stage. He said there would likely be others in the crowd, but not as many as on the stage. He said if he was planning the defense on behalf of God's Own, he would put the individuals with short-range capabilities on the floor, and those with long-range abilities in the crowd. It made sense. We all hoped he was right.

We would split into two groups. I would be in one, Greg in the other. That way each group would have a teleporter in case things went awry. Thread and Dust always worked together and Fin and Greg always worked together. That meant the groups should have been obvious. Fin and Greg on the end of floor with the baptismal pool and less people, and me, Thread, and Dust on the end of the floor with all the people seated in the chairs. We had more active powers and could deal with the larger group more easily.

Fin was hesitant.

"I should be with Hez."

We could all see he wasn't saying it for any tactical reason. I knew I needed to speak up.

"I don't agree with pretty much anything Myrtle said, but I do appreciate how she tries to keep everyone safe. We have to think about our safety now. You and Greg work well together, you know how to have each other's backs. You're bonded like that. The same for Thread and Dust. And me and Vrail. It makes the most sense to put the heaviest hitters where there will likely be the most resistance. Thread, Dust, Vrail, and I should be there. You and Greg should be on the other end of the floor. There is still a handful of people over there, and it's closer to the stage. If the overseer is there, you two can get to him quicker than we can. You can get him. We can get Mom and my brothers. We go in, we get who we can, we get out."

Fin opened his mouth to object, but Greg squeezed his arm

before he could. Then Greg said, "That sounds like the right plan for the situation, Fin. Hez will be fine. You really think Thread and Dust will let anything happen to him? And besides them, Vrail will probably eat everyone before we even make it to the stage."

We talked at length about which beings from the other realms could help. We needed to be able to neutralize any people with abilities in the larger crowd in the bleachers. We needed to be able to fend off long and short-range assaults. We needed to be able to separate my mom, brothers, and the overseer from the rest of the people. And we needed to do it with as few casualties as possible.

After we arranged our lineup, they all went upstairs to change into their special outfits and gear. Greg took Lincoln up with him, and Boon went full size and carried Puff up the stairs. They would be staying with Lincoln while we were all gone.

I used the time to push to the other realms, contact the beings we needed, and arrange the where and when for each of them to show up. I also made a special visit that the others didn't know about. I hope I made the right decision in doing so and that it isn't a mistake. I'm just catching up my journal now so it's as complete as possible. I don't know if I'll make it back, or if any of us will.

Ten

I'll try to remember as much as I can, but I think I'm in shock. I've never been in a situation like we were in the assembly. I don't have the experience that the others have, and I've never been in such a battle before. It wasn't just a fight; it was a battle. And it didn't start the way we expected it to.

We all showed up where we planned. Vrail, Thread, Dust, and I were behind the main seats on the floor, basically between the seats and the bleachers. We wanted to surprise them by showing up behind them. Fin and Greg were on the other side of the floor, between the stage and the baptismal pool. There were various beings from the other realms who all showed up roughly around the same moment we did.

Before we made a step, the overseer was on the microphone, talking to us from the stage.

"Unless you want your friend to die right now, you will send all these creatures back where they came from."

He pressed a button on the podium and Greg fell to the ground, screaming and scratching at the back of his neck.

"If my finger releases this button, that tiny device in his neck will blow through his spinal cord. If any of you make a move, he dies. You didn't think we'd keep him with us all that time and not put in a failsafe, did you? Count yourselves lucky you were out of its tracking range, or we would have found you all long ago."

From across the floor I tried to catch Fin's eye, get some indication of what I should do. But he wasn't focused on me, he was focused on Greg writhing in pain on the ground.

"Five seconds little boy. I'll release the button and he'll be dead."

As he said that last word, his arm disconnected from his body and he screamed. I looked to Thread. Her arms went up as she screamed. "It wasn't me!"

Another slice went through his chest. Another through his throat. A leg fell to the ground. He screamed the entire time. Finally, his head disconnected and rolled off the stage. At that point, Myrtle appeared at the podium, her finger on the button. She had been the extra visit I made, along with Shroud. I wanted her to help us, keep everyone safe, be an ace up the sleeve. She'd taken water from the baptismal pool and made blades to take down the overseer so she could control the button. By that point everyone in the crowd was screaming and running.

Myrtle yelled to Fin, "Get him over here, maybe I can get the thing out of him!"

Everything happened quickly after that. So many were charging us, others were charging for the exits. It was confusing, trying to figure out who was coming for us and who was trying to get away.

In the bleachers I had the snake—I decided to name her Drac, after Dracula, because of her teeth. I also had this fog that dehydrated things almost instantly. One was on either side of the bleachers. As soon as someone in the bleachers exhibited an ability, and there were a lot of them, either Drac or the fog rushed at them and took them down. Some tried to attack them directly, but attacks went straight through the fog and Drac was simply too quick and nimble for them to hit her with anything. People from the bleachers threw all kinds of things at us: fireballs, bolts of electricity, gusts of wind, chairs, tables, other heavy objects.

Most of the time we couldn't even see where they came from. Up above us was a giant bat. It had raised a thin barrier around our two groups, keeping everything from hitting us at once. The bat was our protection from an initial assault from God's Own. The problem was that we needed to move around, especially Fin and Greg, but the shields were stationary and we couldn't pass through them. I called to the bat and had it lower the shields so Fin could get Greg to Myrtle.

Thread and Dust did not hesitate. They tore through the people who ran at us from the floor seats. It was indiscriminate. We didn't try to discern who was attacking and who was fleeing. We knew it might end up like that. Body parts were flying, people were reduced to sand, a few times Thread increased the speed of those running past the point they could control their actions and they slammed into the bleachers and splatted as badly as the fly had on the window. Vrail stayed next to me and ripped apart anyone who got close. I saw that many of them had syringes. They were trying to jab us. Some got close, but none survived the attempt. Next to me I also had the little lizard with the club tongue. He was so low on the ground no one saw him until it was too late, his tongue growing and hitting them, bashing their bones to pieces the way he had the door to the room they were holding Greg in.

I looked over to the stage. Fin had got Greg up there. Myrtle had made a water ball to hold down the button. Greg was face down on the ground and Myrtle kneeled over him, wielding water like a scalpel to dig out the device. I had a giant spider over on their side to offer protection. Instead of shooting silk webs, his were electric. They fried everyone they hit. Those who were able to get in close were lanced by his ample legs or bitten in half by his pincers. From the looks of it, Fin would have been fine without the spider. His sticks were drawn, and he moved through God's Own nearly as quickly as Thread and Dust, without using any abilities. He was so quick. I've never seen someone who could really fight like that. You know, everyone and their mom says *I know karate*, but to see someone who really does know how to fight, it was amazing to watch. I need him to teach me how to fight like that. With him over there, no one was going to lay a hand on Greg or Myrtle.

Drac and the fog had taken down everyone in the bleachers who hadn't run out. Fin was fighting the final two members of God's Own. The rest of the floor was empty, apart from all the pieces of people everywhere. We all ran up to the stage right as Myrtle got the device out of Greg's neck. Myrtle threw the device to the bleachers and released the button. The bleachers exploded.

Greg got to his feet and pressed his hand against the back of his neck to stop the bleeding.

"Myrtle, I had no idea you were so bad ass," Thread said. "Or that you were here in the first place."

"Well, dear, I do what I can," She had that grandmotherly smile. "Fin, Greg, I'm so sorry for how I behaved earlier. It was monstrous of me. I was so shocked by what you were telling me, I just wasn't thinking straight. And I had everyone else in my ear telling me I needed to get you all back with us. I'm so ashamed. Please forgive me."

"You just took down the overseer and saved Greg, I think we can call you forgiven," Fin said as he was placing a bandage on the back of Greg's neck.

I chimed in with," We'll have The Healer fix that up in a bit."

"Thanks, I'd appreciate that." Greg sounded a little worse for the wear after the amateur surgery. "Myrtle, how did you get here? You don't have any other teleporters, and why didn't we see you right away?"

"Well, you can thank young Hezekiah for that. He and his friend over there came for a visit while you were all preparing for this. By the time he came to me, I'd calmed down from our conversation and was in a better place to listen. I thought your chances would be better with me than without me. Hezekiah had a plan to have this little cricket make me invisible so I could be the surprise backup plan."

Shroud popped her head out of Myrtle's pocket and I released her back to her realm.

"Vrail brought me here right after you all," Myrtle went on. "It happened so quickly you probably didn't even notice her doing it. She's very quick, I think."

She had an admiring eye on Vrail.

Myrtle then turned her eye to Fin. "I'm concerned, Fin. There were a lot of people here. There were cameras. This is going to get out. The authorities will come here and find all these bodies. I helped because it was the right thing to do, but this has jeopardized all of us."

I raised my hand like I was back in school. "I actually have an idea about that. And a backup idea if that doesn't work."

"Of course you do," Fin said with a smile.

"I know this is going to be risky, but if we can get rid of all of the bodies and blood here, do you really think anyone would believe what people might say? With no hard evidence, isn't it likely people would just think it's a bunch of religious kooks trying to get attention? If the cameras were on us, but no bodies are found, people will just think it's fake footage. So if we get rid of the bodies and evidence, this is all likely to just blow over as a hoax. And that's if it even gets to that point. The real people running God's Own may not let any of this get out. It might be too risky for them if people like us become common knowledge."

Everyone looked at me. I knew the next question.

"Dear, that would be wonderful, but how do you plan on getting rid of hundreds of corpses and all this blood?" Myrtle asked the question for everyone. "This is a nasty battlefield. A few mops aren't going to cut it."

"That's where I have an idea and a backup idea. However, I need all of you to leave, except Greg. I need his help."

I looked over at Greg as I said it. He had a questioning look on his face.

Before he could ask a question, Myrtle had a statement. "Well, I'm not going anywhere. I'm part of this and I want to know what's being done to fix it."

She had hardly finished her comment when Greg slapped his hand on the floor and a void appeared directly under Myrtle and she fell right through.

Fin gasped. "Where did you send her? She's an older person, a fall can really hurt her!"

"Please, it's OK. I just sent her to her room, her bed specifically," Greg laughed. "Besides, there was no way I was letting her go back to the cabin. I know you noticed, Fin. She had a tracker on her. She already knew where this place was, it's a known property of God's Own. The only reason she'd need a tracker is if she wanted to go to the cabin and find out where it is. We can't let that happen. After all, none of us even know where it is. We should leave it that way. Really, what if they had captured me again, and this time had access to someone with an ability like Drac? Someone who can make us want to tell the truth. We'd all be screwed. The cabin's location is unknown to everyone except Vrail. We should leave it that way."

He made perfect sense. I didn't even know what a tracker

looked like, so I definitely didn't know Myrtle had one.

"I saw it, and I wasn't going to let her go back to the cabin either. But she just saved your life, she might have just saved all our lives. We owe her better than a broken leg if you had just randomly dumped her out somewhere at their new compound."

Fin made as much sense with his point as Greg had with his. Neither was upset. They clearly knew how to communicate with each other in a non-combative way.

"Vrail will take the rest of you back to the cabin," I said, and released all the other beings who had stayed in the place. "This will be OK. I think Greg might be able to deal with all of this, but if the authorities are going to come here, we need to get moving. I can explain this to you all later."

Everyone looked confused, but they trusted me.

"You'll need to take her with you," I pointed to my mom, still sitting in the front row of the seats on the floor by the stage. She hadn't moved during the entire fight. She just sat there and stared forward. My brothers had both run out with the crowd. Fin cringed when he saw her sitting there, probably a flashback to her screaming at us in the street after she left the group. Thread and Dust walked over to her, guided her out of her chair, and walked her over to Vrail.

"Are you sure you want us to take her to the cabin? We can take her somewhere else." Thread remembered that I said I didn't want Mom or my brothers at the cabin.

"No, it's OK, please take her there. There's enough room outside I can call The Healer when Greg and I get back."

I still had a bad feeling about having her at the cabin, but it seemed like the best option at the moment.

Dust held my mom's hand against Vrail, while she and Thread each put a hand of their own against her. Fin kissed me on the forehead and told me he loved me, then he walked to Greg and gave him a more personal kiss and told him he loved him, too. He walked over to Vrail, placed a hand on her, and then they were all gone. Just Greg and I remained.

He looked over the floor, the bleachers, all the carnage. He spread his arms, gesturing to all of it, and said, "Hez, you're a resourceful and creative guy, but if you think I can open a void to get rid of all of this, you're wrong."

"No, I don't think it's that ability that can help us. I think it's your light. Fin told me awhile back that many believe that the abilities most of us have are tied to one of the other beings. That we get access to their ability in some way. Well, I know one of those beings who has an ability remarkably similar to how you described your light blast. I think that maybe it doesn't have the same effect for you as it does her because you don't realize what it can do. If I'm right, it won't affect me, but it might hurt the others. I want you to try something, but it had to be just the two of us."

Back when he described his secondary ability, all I could think of was how I'd watched the Glowing Woman burn away my brother, and then the guards outside Lincoln's detention room with a blast of light.

"And if you're wrong? You said you have a backup idea?"

He didn't believe it was going to work.

"Then I'll call the Glowing Woman herself and see if she can clean up this mess. I think you're the one who said we should all be pushing our abilities right now. This is a chance to do that. I can walk you through it."

If Greg couldn't do it, and the Glowing Woman couldn't do a cleanup on this scale, then I had no idea what to do.

"OK, you're right, let's try this. What do you want me to

do?" He shook out his arms and legs, like he was limbering up for a run.

"When you bring the light, try to keep it here, don't let it just flash. Keep it, feel it, and focus it. Use your hands, like Thread and Dust do sometimes. It might help focus the ability. Start small. If you can keep it here, try to aim it on just a few bodies at first. When you've focused on them, try to intensify it to a burst, but don't let the burst go away. Keep it on those bodies until they fizzle away. If that works, then we'll try to increase the scale."

The logic of it followed. I just hoped I was right.

"And you don't think it'll hurt you? If I can do that, make a light bright enough to burn away this stuff, you think you'll be OK?"

I'm sure the last thing he wanted to do was burn his partner's son out of existence.

"Yeah, I'll be fine. The Glowing Woman's light doesn't work on me. It gets really bright, but it doesn't have any real effect on me."

I really wanted to feel as confident as I made that sound.

With that he turned around and faced away from me. I took a few steps back and lowered my eyes, shielding them with my hand. There was a flash of light. It almost burned out in the first few seconds, but Greg had his hands up and he managed to keep it. Once he had it, it looked easier to hold, like once he knew it was possible, he understood how to keep it harnessed. He directed the light to a few bodies that were close to him. At first, the light stayed at its initial intensity, but then it slowly increased. I could hear Greg breathing. He took long deep breaths. His concentration was growing, and the intensity of the light along with it. There was a quick pulse and the light hit the intensity I'd seen from the Glowing Woman. In seconds it extinguished, and the area where the bodies were, and a few feet surrounding it, were free of any bodily debris.

"What the hell! It worked! Hez, how did you know that would work?" He was like an excited kid discovering something new.

"I really didn't. It was just a guess. I wanted to see if I was right or not. Bet you don't think it's such a useless ability now do you?" I was a little smarmy when I said that.

"No, not at all! This is amazing! Does it only work on dead things, or does it affect living things too?" He wanted to know more.

"I don't know, I've only ever seen the Glowing Woman use it as cleanup after her scream already killed people. Since I don't know, that's why I wanted everyone else to leave, so they wouldn't be hurt if it does burn out living people. I guess that's something for you to keep in mind in any future life or death fight. Do you think you can handle the whole place?"

I wasn't sure how taxing this was for him, especially considering the wound in his neck.

"I think I can, or at least I can try. It wasn't hard at all, once I had it under control. I think I can make it bigger. I think I can make a larger burst to fill this place. Do you want to stay while I try? I can make a void to the cabin for you if you think it might be dangerous."

"I'll stay, I think I'll be fine. I'd rather be here for you."

I wished Fin could have been there to see his partner doing something new and amazing.

With that, Greg walked to the center of the stage, and all I can really say is he lit that place up. I shut my eyes, pulled my shirt over my face, and had my hands covering my eyes, and I swear I still saw the light through all of that. I dropped my hands and shirt and opened my eyes when I heard him jumping up and down on the stage screaming, "Yes, it worked!" over and over again.

He waved me up on the stage.

"Come on! Hurry! Let's go tell everyone! They are not going to believe this!"

As soon as I was on the stage, he opened a void and we met everyone back at the cabin.

Eleven

I didn't say a word as Greg explained what he had done. Everyone congratulated him, hugging, and relishing in the sense of victory and safety. I sat in my chair and looked across the room at my mom, alone on the love seat. She still stared as blankly as she had in the front row by the stage. I knew the look well. It was the same look she would have on her face when I'd peek into her bedroom after she started spending all of her time in there. Not asleep, not awake. Just hollow.

Initially, I didn't notice when the room went quiet. When I did, I looked over at everyone. They were all looking at me. They all looked sad. It was empathy. They cared for me and I was hurting.

"What do you need us to do?" Fin asked.

My mouth opened but the words were slow to come out." We need to get her outside. You all think Vrail is big— she's tiny compared to The Healer. If Vrail is a shed, The Healer is a two-story house. He won't fit in here."

I shook my head. "Sorry. Uh, Fin, Thread, Dust, would you please help get my mom outside? Greg, let's go out there now and I'll call The Healer. He can deal with your neck first. Is anyone else hurt?"

I hadn't noticed until then, but everyone except Greg and I had cleaned up. Everyone had been covered in blood from the massacre at the assembly. Fin was back in dark jeans and a baby-blue polo shirt, Thread and Dust were in floral sundresses. Mom wasn't clean. She looked like she'd soaked in a blood bath. I guess she practically had.

"No, we're all OK," Thread said. "And yes, we'll help her. We'll meet you and Greg in a few minutes."

"Thanks, I appreciate that." I noticed I'd unintentionally gone back to my monotone voice.

Fin and Greg shared a look. It was obvious they were worried about me. I got up, and Greg and I walked out to the yard, the area between the cabin and the water. Vrail followed us out. She hadn't left my side since I got back to the cabin. She's my best friend, and I think I've been spending less time with her since connecting with Fin and the others. I need to change that. She's the one who has been there for me from the beginning, my friend and protector. I put a hand on her forehead after she lowered her head to me. I petted her gently and thanked her for always being with me. She purred and nuzzled.

I lay down on the ground with my head resting on Vrail's leg. I was ready to push, but asked first, "Greg, would you want to come with me? The place where The Healer is, it's beautiful."

"Are you serious? Yes, I'd love to go with you! Those few realms you took Fin and me to were so trippy, I'd love to see more."

It was probably still an adrenaline high from the events of the past hour, but he sounded as excited as a child again.

He lay down next to me and we interlocked hands. I pushed us to Vrail's place, empty while she was with our bodies. I took us to the mountain, with its blue and yellow flakes making blankets of green snow. We walked into the cave. It was the first time Greg saw The Healer.

"Crap! I know you said he was big, but crap! He's huge!"

I kind of like excitable Greg.

From there I asked The Healer to join us behind the cabin, and I took us back to our bodies.

By then, the others were outside with us. Greg popped up and grabbed Fin by the shoulders.

"You have to see this place, it was amazing. It had snow! But it wasn't like our snow, it was different colors, it was so cool."

Fin looked amused while Greg spoke. I'm sure he's dealt with excitable Greg before.

"You are going to be so tuckered out tonight," Fin said, shaking his head.

Greg had a giant grin on his face. "Yeah, I am."

"Greg, are you ready? I don't know exactly what to expect for you." I described what happened last time I called the Healer—not just the healing, but the cleaning and the meditating, too.

"Yeah, I'm ready, let's do this."

He looked like he was limbering up again. He walked over to The Healer and stood in front of him.

The Healer's back was to the water, and this time it seemed like he drew the energy from the water, or maybe from things in the water. He began to glow, the same way he had when he healed me. His eyes slowly opened and beams shone down onto Greg. It only lasted seconds, which made sense. His wound was so small compared to what mine had been. Greg was caked in blood and who knew what else. The Healer raised his hand and Greg elevated off the ground. The Healer's breath cleaned and refreshed Greg's appearance and clothes. He was lowered to the ground, but not into the meditating pose I had been placed in.

Fin, Thread, and Dust looked on in awe. Even after having the process described, it was an entirely different and incredible thing to see.

"That was amazing. I haven't felt this good in a very, very long time. I feel like I've slept for days, and I don't think I've ever felt this clean before," Greg said, looking over himself.

"Let me have a look at your neck," Fin said as he walked around behind Greg. "The bandage is gone, the wound is closed, I don't even see a scar. This is incredible."

Someone had brought down a patio chair for Mom to sit on while Greg was healed. Dust and I lifted her from the seat and walked her over to The Healer. Thread grabbed the chair and brought it over for us to lower Mom into. We all stepped back and waited.

We watched Mom go through the same process Greg had just been through. I hadn't noticed, but Fin had come over and wrapped an arm around my shoulders.

When The Healer was done and lowered Mom back down, he sat her in the chair. No meditating for her either. That surprised me. Given her mental illness and the mind control and the trauma involved in that, I really thought The Healer would put her through that process. Fin and I walked over to her. Everyone else stayed back to give us some privacy.

"Mom, how do you feel? Are you OK?"

"I… I feel fine. I think. I can think. It was hard before. Like being split into pieces, and each piece was fighting the others. But I feel whole again. The other pieces are gone, I think. I feel like me again." She spoke slowly, but she sounded like herself again.

I went to hug her, but she shuddered and pulled away. I was startled by that reaction and just looked over at Fin who had a confused look on his face that mirrored mine. Mom raised herself from the chair. She looked up at The Healer, but spoke to me.

"I know your life has been hard. Harder than it should ever

have been. I'm sorry for that. But when I told you that your power is from Satan, that wasn't someone else speaking. God does not approve of such things. I should not have judged you so harshly, but he will." She looked over to Fin. "I shouldn't have been so angry with you, but you are a sinner, and you will be judged." She was calm as she spoke. The kind of calm that is unnerving.

"Hezekiah is going to come with me. I'll get him help. We will find a way to get Satan out of him." She was still looking at Fin. "And you will not see him again, not unless you give up your sinful ways. He doesn't need your corruptive example in his life."

When she first jerked away from my attempt at a hug, the others had all come over. They heard every word as clearly as Fin and I had. I could tell Greg wanted to send her away, but he hesitated until Fin or I gave the OK. Thread and Dust looked like a mix of sorrow and blood lust. We all had our hope on her being herself again. What we didn't expect was that being a religious zealot was her real self, even if she was a calm one.

"I'm sorry," I said. "I'm truly sorry you feel that way, Dahlia."

I saw a spike of anger at my using her name, instead of calling her Mom.

"Your time as my mom is over. You controlled my past, but my future is with Dad and my new family. It's time for you to leave now. If you have somewhere specific, you'd like to go, Vrail can send you there."

"You listen here, young man," she said, her voice was calm. "You get your things right now. You're coming with me whether you want to or not. I am your mother, and you will treat me with the respect I deserve."

I flicked my eyes over to Greg and gave him a quick nod. He did to Dahlia what he had done to Myrtle, slapped the ground out from underneath her. I didn't bother to ask where he sent her, but I suspect it was the trailer.

I looked over to Fin.

"Dad, I'm sorry. I really thought The Healer would fix things with her. I didn't know that the real her felt this way. I thought those horrible things were coming from the other woman who had controlled her, or her mental illness. I didn't think she would be like this."

He walked over and hugged me tightly." We don't know that she is really like this. We don't know exactly what your friend was able to fix and what he didn't. I don't think this is over, Son."

Twelve

A few weeks have gone by since that last day I wrote about. We've all been taking time to decompress in our various ways. I've grown quite involved with everyone.

Everyday Dad teaches me more and more about chess. I asked him to teach me to fight like he does, but he said it all starts with chess. I don't mind. I've grown to love the game. Also, he hasn't said anything at all about my transition from calling him Fin to calling him Dad, but every time I do, I can see the tiny smile at the edge of his lips. Dahlia may not approve of him, but I couldn't be prouder to call him Dad.

Thread and Dust have been teaching me to swim in the lake behind the cabin. They were appalled when I told them I didn't know how. Even more appalled when I told them I didn't know how to ride a bike either. They've taken it upon themselves to start teaching me the things they say I missed out on in my childhood.

Greg is an early riser like me. When we first came to the cabin, he stayed in his room because he felt awkward around me, since Dad hadn't opened up to me about their relationship yet. After everything was discussed, Greg started joining me on the back patio every morning for coffee. Sometimes we talk, sometimes we sit there quietly and read. When we talk, he tells me stories about himself and Dad. It's a way of letting me get to know them both, what their lives were before I knew them.

I bring Puff and Boon over a few hours every day to play with Lincoln. It's the highlight of his day. I decided not to keep them in our world all the time. They had their own homes and I didn't want to rip them away from that. Greg hasn't decided what to do with Lincoln yet. He's taking time to decide between sending him back to his foster family and keeping him at the cabin with us.

Vrail still stays with me most of the time. Every few days she goes back to her own realm, but only when she wants to. Our bond seems to get stronger all the time. I can feel when she does and does not want to go. It isn't a chore for her to be with me. She wants to stay in my world, and I want her to stay. Every evening the two of us go off in the woods and spend time alone, usually for hours. I talk, she listens, we grow together.

I could never have imagined the life I have now, but I love it all the same. Things may not be perfect, but I'm happy.

There's still a lot to do. We want to figure out if my mom really is beyond our help. I need to find my brothers. I don't feel I owe them anything, but it still feels like the right thing to do to at least make sure they are OK somewhere. We need to reconcile with Myrtle's group. Not join them, but come to an understanding. We may be two separate entities, but we both want to help others like us. We need to stop God's Own. Relatively speaking, the overseer was a small piece of an exceptionally large organization. It was fulfilling for me to see him dead because he had been such a terror in my life. But his death did little to affect that organization. We need to push our abilities, try to reach our full potential. There is going to be a battle coming, one bigger than we've faced before. We have an entire organization to end, and we need to find their founder in the other realms and end him.

We all know the times ahead will be difficult and we don't know what's in store for each of us. For now, we are enjoying a peaceful time, and embracing the opportunity to learn more about each other and grow closer as a family.